A **CARMEN SANDIEGO** Novel

Secrets of the Silver Lion

All rights reserved. For information about permission to reproduce
selections from this book, write to trade.permissions@hmhco.com or to
Permissions, Houghton Mifflin Harcourt Publishing Company, 3 Park
Avenue, 19th Floor, New York, New York 10016.

hmhbooks.com

Designed by Stephanie Hays
The text type was set in Adobe Garamond Pro.
The display type was set in Proxima Nova and Avallon.

The Library of Congress Cataloging-in-Publication data is on file.

ISBN 978-0-358-38067-2

Manufactured in the United States of America
DOC 10 9 8 7 6 5 4 3 2 1

4500802310

A **CARMEN SANDIEGO** Novel

Secrets of the Silver Lion

BY

EMMA OTHEGUY

HOUGHTON MIFFLIN HARCOURT

BOSTON NEW YORK

CHAPTER 1

CARMEN SANDIEGO MOVED SOUNDLESSLY around the deserted terrace, expertly avoiding loose stones and dodging security cameras. In the morning, there would be no evidence that an international thief had been there—Carmen was a pro.

"This place sure is quiet for New York City," Carmen said into her comm-link earring. The terrace was several steps up from the street, and it had been ten minutes since the last car went by. At the far end of the terrace was a stately museum. Carmen thought it looked like a place where someone self-important would live.

The voice on the other end of Carmen's earring was cheerful. Even though they had never met in person, Player was Carmen's best friend. They were partners in fighting VILE (the Villains' International League of Evil) and spoke every single day. Player was always ready with encouragement and quick facts, and now was no different.

"It's the middle of the night, Red. What were you expecting, a welcome band?"

"What ever happened to the city that never sleeps?"

"No one uses this terrace at night. It's all yours, Red — that is, unless our friends show up."

Carmen smiled sneakily to herself. She had reasons to believe that operatives from VILE would be coming to ransack the museum — but with any luck, Carmen would thwart their plans and keep the museum's treasures safe. She could just imagine the faces of criminals like Countess Cleo and Professor Maelstrom, or better yet her archrival Tigress, when they realized that Carmen had beaten them to their prize. Carmen had once been a student criminal-in-training at VILE Academy — ever since Carmen escaped from the academy and started fighting evil, she had tried to stay one step ahead of VILE.

"I think I've found the spot." Carmen focused on a ledge just below a second-story window. It was narrow, but it looked sturdy, and there were no bars on the window.

"Go for it."

Carmen reached into her red trench coat, wound up her arm, and pitched her grappling hook toward the ledge.

"Got it!"

As soundlessly as she had walked around the terrace,

Carmen now shinnied up the rope. When she reached the top of the ledge, she gathered the grappling hook back into her coat and sneaked a peek over her shoulder. The view from above was impressive: to the west, the Hudson River glimmered, and to the south, the lights on Broadway snaked deep into the city. Carmen turned back to the window. It took her two tries to pick the lock before the window finally opened.

Carmen listened for sounds inside, but the museum was empty. She was completely alone.

Still crouched on the ledge, Carmen used her flashlight to figure out where she was. The window opened onto a grand exhibit hall, filled with richly woven tapestries, silver candlesticks, and elegant vases. It wasn't a far jump, and Carmen landed on her feet.

The exhibit hall was packed with stuff VILE would love—she could just imagine Professor Maelstrom melting down those silver candlesticks for cufflinks, like he once wanted to do with an Ecuadorian doubloon. But Carmen knew that VILE was after a bigger prize than the knickknacks in this third-floor gallery. She spotted the stairs and quickly made her way to the ground floor. Luckily, Player had found floorplans, which Carmen had studied carefully.

On the ground floor, Carmen moved toward the front

doors. They were heavy, studded with metal, and secured from the inside with multiple locks. Carmen would deal with those later. Right now, she had one mission.

"Once you get to the doors, it's to your right," Player instructed.

Carmen turned and faced a long, narrow hallway. She shone her flashlight, which illuminated only shadows and a worn stone floor. Past the reach of the light, the hallway continued like a pitch-black tunnel. Carmen squared her shoulders and strode down the hallway, holding the flashlight out in front of her.

A sparkle caught the light. As Carmen neared the end of the hallway, she could just make out a silver shape, about the size of her palm. She drew closer, until she could clearly see that it was a silver carving in the shape of an arrow.

"Do you see it yet?" Player asked into her ear.

Carmen raised her flashlight. She whistled. "I see it."

The silver arrow was nestled into the base of a mahogany throne. The base was intricately carved with scrolls and curlicues, and the legs of the throne were shaped like enormous claws. The arms were fashioned like the heads of two roaring lions. On the seat was a velvet cushion, now threadbare.

"The museum's most prized possession," Player

announced. "It was commissioned by King Felipe IV of Spain in 1621."

"The man clearly had money," Carmen remarked. "But I don't know about taste." The throne was foreboding.

"I think the idea was to intimidate people," Player said. "But that's not why that throne is valuable, it's actually that silver arrow."

Carmen examined the arrow, carefully inlaid on the base of the throne. On either side of it were hollowed out spaces, like molds that were never filled.

"You see the space for the castle and the lion on either side of the arrow?" Player asked. "King Felipe IV also commissioned silver inlays for those spots. They were definitely made, because there are documents confirming it, but somehow the castle and the lion never got to the throne."

Carmen leaned in closer. "The detail on this arrow is amazing. It's almost as if the feather at the end were real. I wish I could see it in proper lighting." She straightened up. "But I need to figure out what VILE is planning."

"Do you, Black Sheep?"

Carmen whirled around, dropping her flashlight in surprise. No one had called her Black Sheep since her days at VILE Academy. Someone flipped a switch, and the hallway was flooded with overhead fluorescents. Carmen covered her face to shade her unadjusted eyes.

"I see our little friend is here," said a singsong voice. "So predictable."

Carmen lowered her hands, still blinking. She gritted her teeth at the person now advancing on her. "I was a year ahead of you, Paperstar, don't call me *little*."

Paperstar smiled sweetly. "But did you *graduate* ahead of me, Black Sheep?" She skipped past Carmen. Her platform patent-leather boots squeaked against the tiled floor. "No, I didn't think so," Paperstar said. "So you see, I think *little* is just the right word for you. *Little* thief. *Little* amateur. Oh, look . . ." — Paperstar hopped onto the throne and crossed her ankles primly — "from up here, little *person*."

Carmen's eyes narrowed. "Get off that throne before I make you, Paperstar."

"As if you could." Paperstar lunged suddenly, throwing an origami star in Carmen's direction. Carmen ducked as the star whipped through the air and sliced past her ear. Now Paperstar emptied her pockets and the paper weapons came faster and faster, thinner and sharper each time. Carmen retreated, ducking, running, and rolling to dodge the stars. At the end of the hallway she turned left and ran, racing through the galleries, taking every turn she could to try and shake Paperstar.

"You'd think those boots would slow her down, but *no*," Carmen shouted to Player, panting as she ran. She hung a sharp left and shrank into the shadows. Paperstar ran past, and Carmen caught her breath as the sound of Paperstar's squeaky boots faded away.

"Player," Carmen hissed into her earpiece, "I've got to get this throne to a secure location—I can't keep it safe here. I think I've got five minutes, tops. Get Ivy—I need backup!" She darted back the way she came and yanked open the door of the first supply closet she found. "Yes, here's a cart!" Carmen grabbed the handle and ran back toward the throne, not even bothering to be quiet. It wouldn't take Paperstar long to figure out where she had gone.

Grunting, Carmen nudged the throne onto the cart. Under her trench coat, she was dripping with sweat.

The front door rattled. *Ivy!* Carmen thought, praying her friend and partner-in-adventure was at the ready. She pushed the cart as hard as she could then leaped onto its base, leaning over the throne like a skier as the cart, the throne, and Carmen hurtled toward the front door. Something sailed across the doorway and Carmen knew Paperstar was back, but if she could just beat her to the door and meet Ivy—

"AAARGH!" Paperstar yelled as she hurtled her body at the cart, pushing it back into the museum and knocking

Carmen to the ground. The doors burst open and Carmen heard Ivy yelling her name.

Seconds later, Carmen heard Paperstar shouting shrilly, "You two get the throne! I'll put Black Sheep out of commission."

Somewhere in the distance, Carmen heard the voices of Le Chèvre and El Topo, two of VILE's top operatives.

Please let Ivy get the throne before them, Carmen said to herself. *Ivy, get the throne!* If she could lead Paperstar away from the museum for long enough — *please get it, please get it!* Carmen reached the window and jumped onto the ledge — with Paperstar only seconds behind.

CHAPTER 2

I VY PUSHED OPEN THE HEAVY DOORS. "I'm coming, Carmen!" she hollered, then stopped in place. A cart loaded with an imposing wooden throne was careening away from the entrance. Not at all the direction they wanted. Suddenly Ivy noticed a flash of red, and then Paperstar, one of VILE's most dangerous villains, leaped off the cart and tore after Carmen, throwing paper darts.

"Come back here!" Ivy shouted. Then she took a second look at the cart and frowned. It looked like VILE had been trying to steal it. And if VILE was taking it from the museum, that could only mean one thing—Carmen would want the throne moved to a secure location. Ivy rolled up her sleeves. Carmen was the VILE expert; Ivy was the gadget expert. And carts were a gadget. She allowed herself one last fist-shake at Paperstar's retreating figure before getting to work. "That's my *friend* you're chasing," she muttered.

A dry voice behind her replied, "And *you're* such a good friend to load up this cart for us."

"Le Chèvre!" Ivy put her hands on her hips, storming back toward the door. Le Chèvre was one of her least favorite VILE operatives—his name meant "The Goat" in French, because he could climb up anything, like a real goat. He had a habit of getting in Ivy's way.

"I was going to climb up the side of the building," Le Chèvre said gleefully. "But now I see that isn't necessary!"

Ivy lunged at the cart, stopping it halfway down the hallway. "You'll have to get past me first," she said.

"Or not," Le Chèvre replied happily. El Topo, another VILE operative, came out of the shadows and appeared at Le Chèvre's shoulder. "Two against one!"

Ivy grabbed the cart with both hands and ran, pushing the cart as hard as she could toward the door. As the heavy throne drew closer, Le Chèvre and El Topo leaped out of the way, and Ivy cheered as the cart cruised through the open doors and into the night.

It would have been a great plan, if the uneven flagstones of the terrace hadn't slowed down the cart. It clunked only a few feet before stopping completely. Ivy had to use all her strength to keep pushing, and the cart moved *slowly*. So slowly that Le Chèvre and El Topo overtook her and wrestled the cart from her. After all, it was two against one.

Ivy put her fingers in her mouth and blew two short whistles as loudly as she could. A New York City bus pulled up, blocking the exit from the terrace.

"Bad news," Ivy called at Le Chèvre and El Topo. "That was the only way outta here."

Le Chèvre pushed the cart to the very edge of the terrace and looked down at the bus. "Hey, driver!" he called. "Get out of our way! Very important museum personnel here!"

Ivy snorted. "Good luck with that. That's not just any bus driver, you know."

As if on cue, a redhead tipped his Red Sox cap at Le Chèvre. He lowered the window and shouted, "Anything I can help you with, sir? Special rates on thrones tonight, system-wide."

The two VILE operatives narrowed their eyes, and Ivy rubbed her hands together. She had them cornered now for sure. The driver was her brother, Zack. He was always there to lend a hand on Carmen's capers, and plus, he had learned to drive just about any vehicle when the two of them were growing up in Boston. There was just one thing Ivy had forgotten—Le Chèvre's incredible climbing abilities. Within seconds he had shinnied up a tree overhanging the terrace and dropped out of sight onto the street below.

"Guess your friend abandoned you," Ivy said to El

Topo. "And guess I'll be taking that back now." She lunged for the cart, but El Topo wheeled it away from her. As she chased him across the terrace, Le Chèvre reappeared carrying . . . a spare piece of lumber?

Ivy stepped closer to Le Chèvre. She did some quick thinking then — "ZACK!" Ivy yelled. "They're going to try and *catapult* it!" She raced after the two VILE operatives, shaking her fist at them. "That thing ain't worth *nothing* if you break it, you clowns!"

But Le Chèvre was sliding the plank under the throne even as she ran, and before Ivy could say "catapult," El Topo was stomping on the other end, and the throne was sailing through the air.

The two VILE operatives took off running with Ivy following close behind. While they climbed up a tree, Ivy hurled herself through the open window of the bus.

"There they are!" Zack shouted. The throne landed softly in a dumpster, sending up a flutter of Styrofoam packing peanuts. "They filled the dumpster with packing peanuts?" Zack said. "I gotta hand it to them, that's some smart thinking. They had to know exactly where the throne would land to pull that off."

"Smart?" Ivy said. "They're taking off with our throne and you're giving them compliments? Look! They're already loading it into a van!" She pointed as Le Chèvre and

El Topo tilted the dumpster and heaved the throne into the back of a van. "Step on it, bro!"

Zack slammed on the gas, but the big bus accelerated slowly while the van zoomed two blocks ahead. Zack leaned over the steering wheel and gritted his teeth, willing the bus to go faster. They sped through two red lights, almost closing the distance between the bus and the van, but as the chase took them farther downtown, the streets filled with cars and pedestrians. So *this* was the city that never slept.

"Slow down, bro, you're gonna hit someone!" Ivy yelled. A group of late-night revelers were crossing the street, singing merrily. Zack slammed on the brakes, and Ivy clutched the bar with both hands as the force thrust her forward.

Zack drummed his fingers impatiently on the steering wheel as people crossed. By the time the street was clear, the van was long gone—and a woman was tapping on the door, waving her bus pass at Zack.

"Uh-oh," Zack said.

"Didn't think someone might actually want to ride the bus?" Ivy asked.

"Planning error," Zack agreed. He opened the door briefly. "Uh—we're closed, miss! No bus service tonight!"

The woman protested, holding up the heavy bags she

was carrying, but Zack yanked the doors closed again. "Sorry, ma'am!" he yelled over his shoulder as the light turned green and he slammed on the gas once more.

"We're too late!" Ivy exclaimed. "They got away from us!"

"What now?" Zack asked, slumping over the steering wheel.

"Zack, *look!*"

Zack pulled over in the bus lane and craned his neck. They were just below the George Washington Bridge, and the trail of lights connecting each pillar looked like Christmas garlands strung with twinkling lights. But that wasn't what Ivy was pointing at. With a squint, Zack made out two dark silhouettes on the top of one of the bridge's high pillars. One of the silhouettes had two buns on each side of her head, and the other wore a fedora and a trench coat.

"Carmen's all the way up there," Ivy said.

The bus lurched forward as Zack pulled a U-turn. Cars honked angrily at him, but Ivy cheered. "We're coming, Carm!"

Zack slammed on the brakes and parked at the foot of the bridge. "We need to send up a signal," he said. "Think fast, sis."

"Let's take a page out of Le Chèvre and El Topo's book and use some leverage." Ivy grabbed Zack's hat off of his head and hopped out of the bus. She found a spare tire kit in the back of the bus and borrowed an inner tube. Then she stood as close under the bridge as she could, loaded the hat into the tube, pulled it as taut as it would go, and slingshot the hat toward Carmen. "Come on, come on, come on," she said to herself.

She watched as it sailed through the sky and descended — right on top of Carmen's fedora.

"Good aim," Zack called from the driver's seat.

And it worked like a charm. Carmen looked down, and Zack and Ivy waved their arms wildly. Carmen unfurled her glider backpack and leaped away from Paperstar, landing on the top of the bus. She army-crawled over to the window and leaned inside.

"Nice getaway vehicle, Zack."

CHAPTER 3

THE NEXT MORNING, THE SPOT where Zack had blocked off the entrance to the museum was now taken up by a police car. In fact, the whole neighborhood was swarming with police cars. Cops in uniform were taking statements from people on the street, and a TV news crew had just pulled up in front of the museum. Everyone was talking about the mysterious disappearance of the Throne of Felipe.

"These thieves were smooth," a news anchor was saying into a microphone. "Detectives have been searching the premises since early morning, but the robbers split without a trace."

"I practically *handed* the throne to them," Carmen grumbled. "I guess we better see if anyone in the museum knows anything."

The museum had a complicated security line after the theft yesterday, but eventually they made their way into the museum and back to the long, narrow hallway, now brightly lit and crowded with people gawking at the scene of the crime. The spot where the throne had been was roped off with police tape. Carmen made her way to the front of the crowd while Zack and Ivy fanned out to look for evidence.

The area where the base of the throne had sat was a slightly different color from the rest of the floor and left a perfect outline of where the throne should be. To Carmen, it looked like the last piece of a puzzle, waiting to be added. She sighed sadly. She had been so close to stopping VILE. Now the throne was probably being sold to other criminals, and Countess Cleo was probably shopping for rubies and diamond earrings.

Someone sighed to Carmen's left, echoing her sadness. Carmen looked up and saw a woman with long black hair. There was a name tag pinned to her blouse. She looked miserable.

"Do you work here"—Carmen stopped to take another look at the woman's name tag—"Milagros?"

Milagros gave Carmen a small smile. "You can call me Milly," she said kindly. "And yes, I'm a curator here. I help plan the exhibits. Although right now I don't really know what I am—I've been working on this throne for years. Now it's gone." She looked like she might cry.

"You don't have any idea who could have stolen it?" Carmen asked eagerly.

"None at all. Of course, the throne had been getting attention last week . . ."

Carmen nodded knowingly. She had been following the news since last Tuesday, when it was announced that one of the missing inlays from the base of the throne had been discovered in Sevilla, Spain. The silver castle, the shape meant to be placed just to the left of the arrow, had been found in a secret vault. A researcher had been exploring the Archivo General de Indias, an enormous library of old documents in Sevilla, when she stumbled upon a trapdoor that led down to a maze of tunnels below the city. No one had set foot in the tunnels for centuries, until this researcher found the trapdoor, and the vault with the missing silver castle.

"The throne on its own is valuable," Milly continued, "because mahogany is expensive wood. And of course silver is costly too. But it's the two *together* that are the real prize for criminals, I think. The throne reunited with its silver inlays would fetch an astronomical sum on the black market. Someone must have heard about them on the news last week—and decided to come steal the throne."

And I know who that someone is, Carmen thought.

Milly stared ahead at the spot where the throne had been. She blinked several times. Hesitantly, Carmen put her hand on Milly's shoulder. "This throne must have meant a lot to you."

"Oh, it's been a fascinating project," Milly said. "The details on the silver arrow were incredible. Some of the finest artistry I've ever seen in silverwork. Even after all these centuries, it's still perfect. You look at the silver arrow and you can almost imagine that it's a real feather on the end."

Carmen felt a rush of affection for Milly. She had thought the exact same thing when she saw the arrow last night. It had been remarkable. There was hardly any time with Paperstar on her tail, but now that it was stolen, she wished she had taken more time to appreciate it.

"The silver castle was supposed to be delivered here from Spain next week," Milly went on, "so that we could attach it to its spot on the base of the throne. I was so looking forward to seeing it."

Suddenly Carmen had a thought that filled her with dread. "Milly!" she said sharply. "Has anyone contacted the people in Spain? If the throne was stolen because of the silver arrow, I can't imagine the same people aren't after the silver castle."

Milly's eyes grew wide. "You don't think—I thought for sure it was a local thief, just someone from New York—"

And I know for sure it was a band of international

criminals, Carmen thought. "This theft was a complicated job," she said. "I wouldn't rule it out. You said it yourself, it's the two together that would be the real prize. Do you know the people who have the castle? Can you get in touch with them and put them on high alert?" Mentally, Carmen was already trying to calculate when the next flight to Spain would be. She couldn't let the silver castle be stolen along with the throne.

"I could," Milly said. "It's on display at the Archivo until next week, when it was supposed to be sent here. I have to go contact them." Looking frantic, Milly started to walk away, then broke into a run.

Carmen was left standing alone, surrounded by people speculating about the theft.

"Maybe they broke in through a window," said a woman in high heels.

"Or they disguised themselves as movers," suggested another.

Carmen shook her head. These theories were getting wilder and wilder. She wondered if the throne had gotten this much interest *before* it was stolen. She pushed through the crowd and headed toward the door. She needed to touch base with Player and get herself to Spain.

Just as she was reaching the exit, someone tapped on her shoulder. It was Milly. She was out of breath.

"I'm sorry," Milly said. "I made the call. They've put

everyone on high alert and are adding additional security. But I meant to ask, I didn't get your name. You've been . . . very kind."

"It's Carmen." She held out her hand, and they shook. "I actually . . . I meant to tell you, I did see the throne before." Carmen didn't mention *when* she had seen it. "It was beautiful. I thought the same thing as you, that the feather at the end of the arrow looked almost real. I'm sorry it was stolen."

"I am too. But I'm glad you appreciated it for what it was worth. And glad you gave me the idea to contact people in Spain — maybe we can save at least one part of the throne."

"Or get it back," Carmen said.

"Dare I hope?" Then Milly asked, "Have you eaten? I'm headed to my lunch break."

Zack appeared as if out of nowhere. "Did someone say lunch? Because I'm famished!" On cue, his stomach rumbled loudly.

"Knock it off, bro," Ivy said, coming up behind Zack. "Carmen's having a conversation here."

Milly laughed. "Are these your friends?" she asked Carmen. "Well, everyone's invited. Lunch is on me."

CHAPTER 4

I T SURE IS NICE TO GET AWAY from that scene," Zack said as Milly led them down the steps of the terrace and away from the museum. "It was packed in there. So many reporters!"

There were fewer reporters on Broadway, but it could hardly be called quiet either. Shoppers went in and out of the stores, wheeling metal hand carts in front of them. Commuters rushed to the bright green posts that marked the subway entrance, then disappeared down the stairwells. People checked their phones at the bus stop or leaned over the curb, scanning the street anxiously for the next bus. Music and good smells blasted out of restaurants.

The group turned onto 155th Street and passed a corner bodega where a man stuck his head out to wave to Milly. A woman pushing a baby stroller approached them from down the street.

"*¿Qué tal?*" asked the woman, kissing Milly's cheek as they drew closer.

"Well, not great," Milly replied. The woman shook her head sympathetically, and Milly pointed to Carmen, Zack, and Ivy. "But I have some new friends to take to lunch today."

"You're in for a treat," the woman said with a wink, before continuing down the street with her baby carriage.

"Milly, do you know *everyone* in this neighborhood?" Ivy asked incredulously. "It's like you're a celebrity!"

"Not quite a celebrity," Milly said, "but I do know a lot of people. My dad was the super for several buildings in this neighborhood when I was growing up. You get to know a lot of people when you're responsible for an entire building, and my dad always took us kids along with him when he went to work on an apartment. By the time I was ten, I think I knew my whole block, although I don't know about the whole neighborhood."

Milly led them into a small restaurant about halfway down the street, where they grabbed a corner table while Milly went to order at the counter. She came back with plates loaded with rice, red beans, plantains, and pork.

"You can get the best Dominican food in town here," Milly said, sliding the plates across the table. Carmen, Zack, and Ivy didn't need telling twice—Carmen realized as soon as she smelled the food that she was hungry after her exhausting and unsuccessful adventure last night.

"It's pretty cool that you get to work in the same neighborhood where you grew up," Carmen said after a few bites, hoping to steer the conversation back to the stolen throne.

Milly nodded. "You could say I've been working on the Throne of Felipe since I was a kid. My father used to bring me to see it all the time, you see."

Ivy whistled. "That's pretty cool."

"Growing up in New York City has its advantages. Whenever my dad had a free afternoon, we would pop into the museum and just stand in front of the throne. We would admire the carpentry, the way the mahogany shone, the details of the silverwork on the arrow. We would play a game where we came up with theories about what happened to the missing castle and lion—like maybe they were stolen by pirates, or maybe they were hidden beneath the seat cushion and no one had bothered to check for hundreds of years. You never know." Milly seemed to cheer up, remembering good times with her dad.

"I bet your dad was pretty excited when they found the missing castle last week!" Zack said.

Milly picked at her rice. "Actually, my dad passed away last year. He would have been thrilled."

"I'm sorry," Carmen said. "It must make you sad that he couldn't be here to find out."

"Just yesterday I had gotten the green light to loan the throne, with the missing silver castle attached, to a special exhibit in Bolivia—I think that would have meant a lot to my dad."

Zack scarfed down a forkful of plantains. "Wait a second. I thought you said your dad liked to visit the throne at the museum. Why would he want it to go to Bolivia—that's all the way in South America!"

Milly laughed. "My dad was from Bolivia. This neighborhood, Washington Heights, is home to many Latino immigrants like my dad. And in a way, the throne is also Bolivian."

"I thought it was commissioned by the king of Spain?" Ivy asked.

"It was," Milly said. "But the silver arrow, castle, and lion weren't made in Spain. The chair was made by carpenters for Felipe's Spanish palace, with precise specifications about where the three silver inlays would go. But the silver shapes themselves were made by expert silversmiths in the city of Potosí, in Bolivia. It's high up in the Andes Mountains."

"We know about the Andes," Zack said. "And the elevation up there! Once we were in Ecuador for a caper—"

Ivy elbowed Zack hard, and he stopped midsentence. "A caper and a tuna!" Ivy finished for him. "Tuna is very big in Ecuador."

Luckily Milly didn't seem to notice. "The air is so thin in the Andean highlands that it's easy to get sick if you're not careful," she said. "Especially if you're used to life at sea level. Although I'm a little jealous that the three of you have gotten to visit the Andes. I've never been, even though it's my father's homeland. This special exhibit was going to be the first time I got to go."

"And now VILE ruined everything," Carmen muttered under her breath.

Milly sighed again. "My dad used to say that the throne represented our family. See, my mom is Spanish and my dad is Bolivian—just like parts of the throne were made in Spain, but parts were made in Bolivia. Come to think of it," Milly added, "the lumber for the throne probably came from trees in the Caribbean—which is where a lot of our neighbors in Washington Heights are from. So it really did represent us." She looked at the three faces across the table from her. "I don't really know why I'm telling you all this. Where are you all from?"

"Boston," Zack said proudly, tipping his Red Sox cap and pointing to Ivy and himself.

"I don't know where I'm from," Carmen said hesitantly.

"I'm an orphan, technically." She struggled for words to explain without giving away too much of her identity. "My adoptive—well—my adoptive family"—she nearly choked out the word, since the VILE faculty could hardly be considered family—"they found me near Buenos Aires, Argentina, when I was a baby. But I've never been there, and I don't know anything about my life before I was adopted."

Milly's face was filled with sympathy. "Don't you ever wonder what it would be like? To go to this place—this place you've heard of but have never been? I've dreamed about Bolivia since I was a kid, and ever since I could read, I've learned as much about it as I could. My dad always talked about it, but we could never afford to go—it's such a long flight—now with the museum paying for my trip, it was going to be my first chance."

Carmen nodded slowly. She understood what Milly meant. She tried not to think too much about where she came from, because she wanted to focus on fighting VILE and stopping their evil crimes. But sometimes thoughts about her mysterious origins crept up on her. Like now.

"It's not fair that you missed your chance to go there," Carmen said. "To really find out where you come from."

"I've been telling myself all week that it would be like a little piece of my dad got to go home. It made me happy—thinking that those silver shapes were going back to where they came from, and I was going back to where my dad came from."

As Milly spoke, Carmen felt angrier and angrier at VILE. Not only had they made it impossible for her to know where she really came from, now they had made it impossible for Milly to get to know the place where her dad's family was from. "Milly, we're getting you that throne back," Carmen said through gritted teeth. "You can count on it."

CHAPTER 5

*P*APERSTAR SKIPPED INTO THE FACULTY ROOM and curtsied cutely in front of the table. She had been reprimanded by VILE faculty in this room more than once, but today they were singing her praises. The throne she had successfully stolen (with a little help from Le Chèvre and El Topo) had been positioned behind the faculty table. Countess Cleo was now settled comfortably in it.

"Good work, champ," Coach Brunt congratulated her.

"I must say, this chair suits me well," said Countess Cleo, crossing her ankles and folding her hands.

"Ha! 'Chair'!" Coach Brunt laughed heartily at Countess Cleo's joke.

"Don't get too comfortable there," Professor Maelstrom said. "We are planning to sell it, aren't we?"

Countess Cleo tsked. "How could you ask, when I was the one who found you a buyer? The Spanish billionaire

Salvador de Burgos has offered to pay a small fortune for the throne and the three silver inlays. He thinks it will look just stunning in the private study of his mansion in Sevilla."

"Might I point out a flaw in your otherwise airtight plan?" Professor Maelstrom said condescendingly. "We only have *one* inlay."

"The silver castle will be easy to steal," Countess Cleo said. "You've seen the news. They found that vault beneath the Archivo General de Indias and the castle was just sitting there. And the fools put it on display. So that the public could 'enjoy it.' Just asking for someone to walk in and take it."

Professor Maelstrom was unimpressed. "That's only two out of three."

Countess Cleo picked a spot of fuzz off of her cashmere shawl. "Dr. Bellum?"

Dr. Bellum tapped the screen in front of her. "I've secured high-definition security footage from the vault in Sevilla where the silver castle was found!"

"Yes, but do any of those videos you've wasted days hacking tell us anything about the silver lion," Professor Maelstrom replied, "which is the rather glaring flaw in this mission?"

Dr. Bellum pinched the screen, zooming out to an overview of the tunnel system. "The tunnels are vast and full of vaults and hidey-holes. If the castle was in one vault, we have every reason to believe the lion will be somewhere down there too, and not far from where the castle was found."

Paperstar hummed a little tune to herself. Meetings bored her. She just wanted to fold paper and stop Carmen, which were the two things she did best, in her own opinion.

"If the lion is really in that maze, I'll be shopping for a solid gold watch by Monday." Professor Maelstrom finally cracked a smile.

"If we steal the silver castle and find the silver lion, that lump of wood is basically priceless," Coach Brunt agreed, nodding toward Countess Cleo and the throne.

Dr. Bellum rubbed her hands together and turned back to her screens.

"Very well," Professor Maelstrom replied. "Our two tasks are clear. Steal the castle; find the lion." He turned to Paperstar and sized her up. "Ready for your next mission?"

Paperstar rocked back and forth on her platform boots. She was ready.

CHAPTER 6

BEFORE CARMEN LEFT THE MUSEUM that evening, Milly reported back that the Archivo had moved the silver castle to a top-security display case with motion sensors, fingerprint collection, and hidden cameras. There were guards outside the building and at the entrance to the underground tunnels. No one with any sense would try to rob it. *Not that VILE has any sense,* Carmen thought. But still, she walked down the steps of the terrace feeling optimistic: she and Player would come up with a plan to rescue the throne, Milly would get to take her trip to Bolivia, and the silver castle would remain safe.

Carmen stopped in a bagel shop as soon as she woke up the next morning. Everyone said that New York City bagels were the best in the world, and she was eager to try one out. It was a little place with an orange awning, a few blocks from the museum. There was a long line, cramping everyone between the drinks refrigerator and the bagel counter. Other people were scrolling on their phones or watching the television on the wall, which was playing a morning talk show. But Carmen never wasted an opportunity to gather potential clues. She studied each and every face on the line and noted what they were reading—you never knew who VILE had gotten to aid and abet in their crimes. But she didn't find anything suspicious.

Just as Carmen was getting to the front of the line, the morning talk show flashed a photo of a small object, tarnished but unmistakable: the silver castle. Carmen stopped in place to watch the television.

"Hey!" the cashier barked. "What's your order?"

But Carmen was transfixed. She watched as the screen flashed back to the talk show.

"Another theft."

"Two in a row."

"These must be international criminals—first New York City, now Sevilla—this is a global crime scene now."

Carmen felt like the wind had been knocked out of her. The silver castle had been stolen from its high-security display case in Spain—and the Spanish police didn't have a clue who had done it.

"Come on," the cashier urged, "you're holding up the line!"

Carmen snapped out of it. "Sorry—not hungry anymore!" She left the line as people shouted at her for holding them up, then ducked out of the bagel shop. She ran as fast as she could toward the hotel to tell Zack and Ivy what had happened.

"Player!" she called into her earring. "Turn on the TV! And book us a flight to Spain!"

She was so distracted that she practically collided with Milly, who was coming down the block from the other direction.

"Did you hear?"

"Just got the news," Milly said, out of breath. "I was going to the police station—"

"Milly," Carmen said, interrupting her, "what information can you give me on those underground tunnels in Sevilla? I need whatever you can possibly find. Who built them, what for, and why were they hidden?"

"You're not . . . you're not just an art lover, are you? You're . . . are you an undercover agent, or something?"

Carmen turned away. She wanted to tell Milly who she was, but she couldn't risk letting anyone interfere with her plans. Not the police, and not the museum. "I'm . . ." she said, biting her lip. "I'm someone who can help. I wish I could tell you more. But I need you to trust me."

"Look at me."

Carmen turned back toward Milly, and they locked eyes.

"Okay," Milly said, taking a deep breath. "Shake on it."

They shook.

"Ready for a private tour?" Milly said.

"I'll call Zack and Ivy."

Carmen, Zack, and Ivy followed Milly to her office, which was tucked behind a panel of wool tapestries on the second floor. The office was cramped with file folders and binders, but Milly's tiny desk was neatly organized. On the desk was a computer, a framed picture of a smiling man, and next to it a single flower in a vase.

"Have a seat," Milly said, although the only chair was at her desk. Zack made do by perching on a stack of folders.

"Not that much is known about the tunnels," Milly said, "since they were just discovered. But I've been talking to my friends at the Archivo General de Indias—"

"I'm sorry, the *what?*" Ivy asked.

"Oh," Milly said, "I forget you don't know. An archive is like a library for handwritten documents and important papers. The archive where the tunnels were found—it's called the Archivo General de Indias, which means 'The General Archive of the Indies'—meaning the Americas. When the Spanish Empire colonized Latin America, they called the whole region 'the Indies.' Today, all the records from that time period are kept in the Archivo General de Indias—AGI for short."

"Got it," Ivy said.

"Back to your friends at the AGI," Carmen said. "What did they tell you? Have they explored the tunnels more since the silver castle was found?"

"Oh, they've been tearing them apart!" Milly said. "But it's a shocking discovery, and it will be ages before they've explored the whole network of tunnels. Researchers have to be very careful down there—the tunnels were probably built hundreds of years ago, and there are places with cave-ins, or where water has gotten in. And of course, it's a total maze—anyone down there has to have a plan to avoid getting lost, or they could be stuck for days."

"How could no one have found the tunnels before now?" Carmen asked. "Wouldn't the electric company have found them when they were laying new power lines?"

"Not necessarily," Milly said. "These are very, very deep underground. Far below where any power lines or plumbing would be." She logged in to her computer and turned the screen to face them.

They all leaned forward to look at the picture on the screen. It was the longest flight of stairs Carmen had ever seen, and in the background the stairs melted into nothing. It was like they led to a black hole.

"This is just the first flight of steps down into the tunnels," Milly was saying. "There are two more flights of stairs like this on the way down. There's very little light, and the steps are old and uneven."

Milly put her chin in her hand and flipped through more pictures of stairs. "It will be years before they've explored the whole place."

"But do they know who built it?" Carmen asked. "It must have taken a lot of work to dig that deep—and in the seventeenth century!"

"No power tools back then, that's for sure," Zack added.

"Or dynamite, for that matter," Milly said. "These tunnels were surely dug by hand."

Zack whistled.

Carmen shook her head. Who would go through that much trouble to dig a maze of tunnels—only to have them boarded up, unknown to the rest of the world?

"The archivists at the AGI suspect it was a very wealthy merchant who had them built," Milly went on. "Before the building became an archive, it was a merchants' exchange. Plus, the vault was full of expensive treasures—its contents make our collection here in New York look pitiful."

"You do have some nice candlesticks and tapestries," Ivy said soothingly.

Milly showed them a picture of the vault. It looked

small, barely big enough for one person to stand in, but it was filled with shelves, each packed tightly with gold and silver that was still, somehow, shining after all these years. There was jewelry too—chokers studded with gemstones and what looked like a diamond bangle.

"They're *very* nice tapestries," Ivy added. Everyone laughed.

"They can keep their fancy jewels," Milly said. "I just want the throne back. It makes me so angry, thinking that criminals could be selling it on the black market as we speak."

"Milly can you send me those pictures?" Carmen asked quickly. "We have a plane to catch."

CHAPTER 7

YOU'RE ALL SET, RED!"

Carmen pulled out her flight app and, sure enough, there were the tickets for her red-eye flight. She and Zack and Ivy boarded the big plane, where they had seats next to one another in the main cabin. Carmen and Ivy gave Zack the aisle so he could try and get a peek at the cockpit. "I've always wanted to fly one of these things!" he kept saying. "It's like a mega-bus in the air!"

Carmen was used to sleeping on planes, so she nodded off. When she opened her eyes, the first thing she saw were pink fluffy clouds out the window. It was morning in Europe, and the plane would be landing soon.

The pilot's voice came over the plane's crackly loudspeaker. "Weather in Madrid, Spain, is eighty-five degrees Fahrenheit, twenty-nine degrees Celsius, sunny, and dry. Flight attendants, please prepare for landing."

"Where to next, Carm?" Zack asked once they had touched down and deplaned.

Player rattled off directions through Carmen's earring. "You've just landed in Madrid, which is the capital of Spain. Fun fact: King Felipe II picked Madrid to be the capital of Spain five hundred years ago because it's smack dab in the middle of the country. Before that it was just a little town."

"The same King Felipe who commissioned the throne?" Carmen asked.

"Nope," Player replied. "Different guys. The throne was commissioned by King Felipe *IV*—that was two kings later."

Carmen shook her head. "You'd think they would come up with a different name!"

"Sevilla, where the silver castle was stolen, is three hundred miles south of Madrid."

When Carmen told that to Zack and Ivy, they groaned.

"That's not going to be a short trip," Ivy complained. "Someone'll get carsick."

"Luckily," Player explained, "Spain has some of the speediest trains in the world. These trains regularly go one hundred and ninety-three miles per hour—that's nearly three times as fast as a car! You'll be there in no time."

Player was right. Once they were in the train, it was smooth sailing. The train was sleek and modern, and it was so quiet you hardly noticed it zooming down the tracks. It was only when Carmen looked out the window and saw that the landscape was a blur that she realized how fast they were going. Still, even from the blur she got a taste of the dusty tans and sage greens of the Spanish countryside. She could hardly believe it when they pulled into the train station in Sevilla, only two and a half hours after they had left Madrid.

They wasted no time heading to the AGI. The walk there took them through a plaza, a main square paved with tan and brown flagstones. Little kids were running around playing tag, and two older women sat on a park bench. It was nearly 100°F (37°C) outside, and Ivy fanned herself while Zack complained loudly. Thankfully they turned onto a narrow street, which was shady, before ending up at another plaza, this one dominated by a two-story building. It was rectangular and reddish-brown with a fanciful turret in each corner. Palm trees framed the entrance.

It should have been a tourist magnet, but police tape covered the doorway and several of the windows.

"We seem to be running into a lot of this lately," Ivy remarked, nodding toward the police car parked on the far side of the plaza.

Carmen checked the policeman in the car. He was scrolling on his phone and didn't seem to be paying much attention to the scene at the AGI. "Wait here," she said, and before anyone could stop her, she ducked under the police tape and pushed open the door to the Archivo.

Inside, it was very quiet. "Player, are you there?" Carmen whispered. "I'm going to look for that trapdoor."

"I'm with you, Red," Player replied. "Keep an eye out for staff—just because the police closed the AGI to the public doesn't mean someone who works there doesn't pop in."

"I'll be careful, but it's pretty deserted." Carmen almost wished she'd brought her trench coat and tools with her; now would be the perfect time to send Red Drone to explore the tunnels. But she couldn't waste this chance to gather information while the policeman was distracted.

Her footsteps echoed down the tile hallway. There were high arched ceilings overhead, and at the end of the hallway, a cannon faced her. "Welcoming," Carmen said sarcastically.

"I think they were going for grand and elegant," Player explained. "This building was originally built as a merchants' exchange, under King Felipe II."

"Same one who picked Madrid on a map?"

"You're getting the hang of this. King Felipe II built this place as a merchants' exchange because the merchants used to sell their stuff in the back of the cathedral, and the bishops didn't exactly like that."

"I can't imagine they would have."

"But the merchants didn't want to do their buying and selling outside, because in case you haven't noticed, it's *hot* in Sevilla!"

Carmen hastened her footsteps. "So, one of the merchants back then must have built the secret maze. It would have been great for him — he had the most secure vault in the world, and then, whenever he had a buyer for one of his knickknacks, he could just go get it. People probably thought he was some kind of genius, but really he was just running down the stairs!"

"It's as good a theory as any," Player said.

At the cannon, Carmen turned right and found herself in a high-ceilinged room, and at the center of the room was a glass display case.

"How does it look?" Player asked.

"Empty. They must have figured out a way to disable the alarms before breaking into it. Leave it to VILE."

Carmen turned onto another hallway, this one full of paintings.

"Oh, did you get to the Felipes?" Player asked.

"These old guys?" Carmen paused in front of the row of paintings, each one in a gilded frame. "How'd they get to be kings?"

"It's called a dynasty, Red. They were just born. What are the paintings like?"

"They're . . . well . . . let's just say the painter did a great job capturing the light."

Player made a snorting noise. "The Felipes weren't known for being attractive. More like, for having long chins."

"These are *very* long chins. I still think they should have gotten their own names, anyway."

Carmen turned her attention away from the wall and to the floor. She walked slowly, paying attention to any inconsistencies on the ground. "I think I found it," she said finally.

A little patch of the floor had been cordoned off with velvet rope, and a sign in front of it read *¡Aviso!*

Carmen reached under the velvet rope and pulled and prodded and pushed every one of the stones on the trapdoor. There was no visible ring or lever, and she had no idea how it opened. Finally she gave it a good hard kick, and the trapdoor sprung open, revealing the endless flight of stairs Milly had shown them in pictures.

"Wish me luck," Carmen said under her breath. Player must have been holding *his* breath, because he didn't reply.

Carmen tested each step by reaching her foot out and tapping it before putting any weight on it. When she was halfway down the first set of stairs, she heard footsteps overhead.

"Uh-oh. We've got company," she said.

"*¡No es justo!*" a man was shouting. "It's not right!" he carried on in Spanish. "Just because the police want to investigate does not mean research stops! I must return to my manuscripts!"

"Paco," said a woman's voice soothingly, "now is not the time! The police have promised they'll reopen the Archivo tomorrow. Then you can return to your work. Just one day."

"One day? Would I ask you to give up breathing for one day? I am a historian, I breathe the documents of this archive and work must not stop, even for one day!"

Carmen pressed herself against the stone wall, hoping they didn't come near the trapdoor.

"*Ay, pero, Paco,*" the woman complained. "Don't you want to go to Salvador de Burgos's house? How often does a multibillionaire give tours of his private mansion?"

"Pilar, I do *not* want to go to the tour of de Burgos's house. Just because he has the most impressive collection of seventeenth-century art, including treasures I have studied at length and only dreamed of seeing, and just because this is the one and only opportunity to see that collection does *not* mean I want to go! I will not be deterred from my work!"

Carmen would have given up on Paco a long time ago, but Pilar continued cajoling, "*Paco, mi amor,* it's a once-in-a-lifetime opportunity. Salvador de Burgos has generously offered to let the public tour his treasures, since we are all in mourning for the loss of the silver castle. Let's leave the Archivo until tomorrow and go see the tour."

But Paco was stubborn. "Pilar, you must do what you want. But *I* am going up the stairs to work in my office."

"*¡Señor!*" came another man's voice. "We must ask you to leave the premises immediately. This is an active police investigation!"

Carmen groaned. "Lunch break's over, I guess."

There was a lot of commotion upstairs, then silence.

"Red?" Player whispered.

Carmen strained to hear. There were footsteps and voices echoing from different parts of the building, but none of them clear enough to hear. It seemed everyone had moved away from the trapdoor.

"Gotta go," Carmen said. "Coast is clear."

She dashed up the stairs and pushed the trapdoor up with her shoulder. She looked right and left. The hallway was empty, but she saw a pair of shiny black boots milling around the room with the high ceiling.

"You're not going to keep searching the tunnels?" Player asked.

"No point now, not with the police everywhere. But I'll tell you where I *am* going. What's the deal with that Salvador de Burgos character?"

CHAPTER 8

T HIS BERET MAKES MY HEAD ITCHY!" Zack complained.

"Quit it, bro," said Ivy. "We need to look like art students." She was wearing a paint-splattered smock and black leggings.

Carmen adjusted the sketchpad she was carrying under her arm. They were trying to blend in with the throng of history buffs and art aficionados who had surrounded the entrance to Salvador de Burgos's mansion. The tan house blended in with the streets of Sevilla, and it was so elaborate that it was more like a small castle than a mansion.

Two men in black suits pushed through the line.

"I heard those are de Burgos's personal bodyguards," Ivy hissed. "Don't mess with those guys!"

Once they got in, the inside of the mansion was even more impressive than the outside. Everything was made of marble: the floor, the stairs, and the artfully sculpted pillars. Unfortunately, you weren't allowed to explore on your own — Carmen, Zack, and Ivy had to join a tour. The guide was a short man who droned on and on, explaining how the artist's perspective affected each statue and why there were five birds on a particular tapestry. Carmen tried to look like someone who cared, but it took effort. The guide spoke in a monotone.

They stood in front of one ceramic vase for what seemed like an eternity, and the guide's voice was practically lulling Carmen to sleep. Her eyes were drooping when she noticed a man in a delivery uniform walking through with a hand truck. It was loaded up with a box the size of a refrigerator.

The delivery man stumbled over the corner of the rug and lunged to catch the box before it fell. He just managed to steady it in time, but the noise interrupted the tour. Except for the guide, everyone welcomed the distraction.

"Perdón," said the delivery worker. "Just a . . . a new refrigerator for Señor Salvador!"

The guide nodded and returned to how many brass candlesticks some Felipe or other had owned, as if nothing had happened. Carmen, however, stepped closer to Ivy.

"What is it, Carm?" Ivy asked quietly.

"Cover for me," Carmen replied in a whisper. "And stall the tour until I get back. Ask about the Felipes' chins if you have to."

Ivy nodded, and Carmen slipped away.

The delivery man was now bumping the refrigerator box up a set of marble staircases on the far side of the mansion. It looked like hard going. Carmen hung back in the shadows until he was at the top of the stairs, then followed him. He wheeled the box through room after room packed with elaborate artwork before disappearing behind a wooden door. Carmen inched along the wall, then peered slowly around the corner of the doorframe.

The room was carpeted in plush red velvet, and a portrait of Salvador de Burgos hung over an oak wood desk. Carmen examined the painting. De Burgos was short and bald, with a very straight nose and thin lips. His chin could give the Felipes a run for their droopiness.

Bookshelves covered every available wall. There were no windows, and only one desk lamp. It was clearly some sort of study.

Who puts a refrigerator in their study? Carmen thought.

The man turned around suddenly, and Carmen yanked her head back. She listened for sounds, but the delivery worker was clearly frozen in place. He must have sensed her presence. "Who's there?" he called.

Carmen stayed silent.

"This place is spooky," the worker muttered to himself. Then Carmen heard the refrigerator box clang against the back of the hand truck, and the man was moving again.

Only he didn't come out the way he had gone in. And if Carmen remembered correctly—and she was pretty sure she did, since she always scanned rooms carefully as part of any reconnaissance—there were no other exits.

Slooowly, Carmen peered around the door again. She watched as the man did something with his hand by one of the bookcases. There was a *ping!* and then suddenly the entire bookcase swung outward like a door, and bright daylight shone through.

So that's Salvador de Burgos's private study! Carmen waited until the man had swung the bookcase shut behind him, then darted inside. She crossed the room in three quick steps and examined the trick bookcase. The books had titles like *Treasures of the Seventeenth Century* and *Spanish Art for the Rich and Famous* and were bound in rich brown leather and embossed in gold.

Carmen tried pulling a book off the shelf, but it wouldn't budge. They were real books, but someone had gone and cemented them in place somehow. She felt along the edges of the bookcase. There were grooves running in two parallel lines around the edge of the bookcase.

She slid her fingernails along one of the grooves until it snagged on something. Carmen pulled back her arm.

Hesitatingly, she reached out her arm again and put her fingernails back in the place they had been. A tiny button, no bigger than the point of a pin, was hidden in one of the grooves. Carmen pressed down and—

Ping!

CHAPTER 9

FOUR STUNNED FACES TURNED toward Carmen. There was the deliveryman, one hand still on the refrigerator box, the two bodyguards dressed all in black, and Salvador de Burgos himself.

Salvador de Burgos looked like he was about eighty years old; much older than when his portrait had been painted. Now he was bald, his posture was stooped, and tufts of white hair sprouted from his ears. If it hadn't been for his silk suit and elegant red pocket square, you would have never guessed he was an extremely rich art collector.

Carmen calculated her options. No one had moved, but she guessed she had about thirty seconds before the bodyguards decided to attack. It was too late to hide and convince everyone they were seeing things. She was standing in the middle of the doorway! *So much for never entering a room without an exit plan,* Carmen thought. *Coach*

Brunt would be furious. Her only option was to run. She turned around but—

"Petra!" cried de Burgos. "*¡Qué bueno que llegaste!* Come here, girl!"

"Err," Carmen said. "I—" Something brushed by her feet. She looked and saw a shaggy, lap-size dog with bright yellow booties on each of its feet. Carmen bent down and scooped up the dog.

"Petra was barking," she said in what she hoped was very convincing Spanish, "so I brought her up. She seemed lonely!"

The bodyguards narrowed their eyes, but if Salvador de Burgos thought it was unusual that his dog had been delivered to his secret study by a complete stranger, he didn't say anything. Instead, he grabbed Petra and kissed her face all over, laughing at the wet kisses Petra gave in return.

"How long have you been working here?" Salvador de Burgos asked Carmen in between dog slobbers.

That explained it. Salvador de Burgos thought Carmen was household staff. That's how many servants he had.

Carmen leaned casually against the side of the doorframe. "About a month, sir. I don't usually handle the upstairs rooms, but since Petra has taken to me so well . . ."

Salvador de Burgos kissed the dog even more. "*¡Ay,*

mi amor! Do you like the nice girl? *Sí, yo creo que sí,* yes, you do."

Carmen took advantage of de Burgos's distracted state and sneaked a peek at the deliveryman, who had loaded the refrigerator box off the hand truck and was making his way toward the door. Carmen cocked her head to the left, trying to see the shipping label on the box, but it was too far away.

Carmen changed strategies. "Petra's booties are quite impressive, were they handmade?" She stepped closer to de Burgos. Just a few more inches, and she would be able to see the shipping label.

"*¡Claro que sí!*" said Salvador. "Nothing but the finest calf leather for my *amorcito.* The leather was expertly dyed by fine artisans in the Pyrenees and fitted to size by a master tailor in Madrid. I wouldn't dream of putting just any leather on you, would I, *mi reina?*"

De Burgos was talking to the dog again.

The deliveryman tipped his hat and left the room without saying anything. The refrigerator box was now sitting under the window, and the silent bodyguards moved in front of it. *Interesting,* Carmen thought. *I'm betting those bodyguards aren't guarding bodies right now — they're more worried about that refrigerator box.*

Carmen cleared her throat and addressed de Burgos. "I've always been interested in, um, hand-dyed leather from the Pyrenees. It is after all, the finest leather. Everything in your house is the finest."

De Burgos finally set down Petra and looked at Carmen. "You appreciate my treasures?"

"Oh yes!" Carmen said (which was true). "That's the reason I wanted to get a job here. I'm an art student," she added (this was false).

Now Salvador de Burgos came alive. Suddenly he was sharp and alert, and Carmen remembered that before he was an old dog-loving billionaire, he had been a shrewd and ruthless businessman. He stepped closer to Carmen. "What type of art interests you, young lady?"

"I'm interested in seventeenth-century silversmithing. It's my longtime passion." Pushing her luck, Carmen added, "I've been following the Throne of Felipe story. To think I almost had a chance to see the silver castle with my own eyes but missed it!"

"I went," de Burgos said, almost hungrily. "I'm a patron of the Archivo, so I had a private viewing yesterday, before the theft. The castle did not disappoint. The artistry!"

"I heard that the castle was made with seven different molds, hand poured and detail carved."

"Did you know the artisan who carved the arrow worked for thirty hours uninterrupted, not sleeping or eating so as to perfectly achieve each hair of the feather?"

Poor man, Carmen thought. "You must have seen so much amazing silversmithing in your lifetime," she said, encouraging de Burgos to continue.

"I have!" he replied, waving his hand around the private room. It was like a minimuseum. The walls were filled with velvet cushions, each one displaying a precious gemstone, a silver bauble, or a gold treasure. "This is where I keep the prizes of my collection. Prizes too great to be shown to anyone but my most *trusted* household staff."

The word *trusted* seemed to wake up de Burgos. He coughed. "How long did you say you have been working here, dear?"

"About a month. But like I said, Petra has taken a liking to me." As if on cue, Petra trotted up to Carmen and allowed herself to be scooped up. When Carmen petted her behind the ears, she snuggled into her arms happily. Carmen was going to buy this dog the biggest bone in Sevilla as soon as she got out.

"Perfecto, qué bueno," de Burgos said to himself. "Well, in that case—"

"Señor, you were telling me about your collection? I'm very interested, of course, being an art student and all."

"My collection! Oh yes! This is the finest collection in the country. Or the hemisphere. Or the planet, I should think! But the Throne of Felipe—now that would be the crowning glory."

"The woodwork is stunning," Carmen said, goading him on.

De Burgos shook his head. "That's what people don't understand about the Throne of Felipe. There's nothing valuable about a wooden chair, and while each of the silver inlays is lovely in its own right, the real value is in the *combination*. You see, long ago, our country was divided into many kingdoms, before powerful queens and kings forced the different kingdoms into submission and formed one unified Spain."

Carmen drew her head back. "Um, didn't the people mind being forced into submission?"

De Burgos made a fist. "It didn't matter. They were weak, and the monarchs were strong."

"And this all has to do with the throne because . . . ?" De Burgos was starting to freak her out.

"Each of the inlays represented one of the old kingdoms. An arrow for the Kingdom of Aragón. A castle for the Kingdom of Castilla. And a lion"—Salvador made a claw and gave a mini roar—"for the Kingdom of León. Together, they represent the power and might of the Spanish crown over all other places!" De Burgos was flat-out giddy now.

Carmen stepped away from him. "That's . . ." *horrible,* she thought. *Apparently he thinks it's terrific for kings and queens to "force people into submission."* "That's very nice," she finished.

But de Burgos wasn't done talking. He moved closer and closer to Carmen, forcing her to retreat closer and closer to the doorway. "If the throne were reunited with all three silver inlays — it would have to be *all three,* mind you, because two would not be nearly valuable enough — we would be talking about a priceless artifact. Priceless. Worth beyond measure! It would sell on the black market for ten times every treasure in this house combined."

"That's a lot of money," Carmen replied, holding Petra a little tighter.

Salvador de Burgos shook his head. "Of course, I would never sell such an object on the black market. I would just want to admire the silversmithing."

Carmen was ready to make her exit. She put her finger to her ear as if she had just heard something. "They're calling me downstairs! Got to go!"

She tossed Petra into Salvador de Burgos's open arms and ran down the stairs, hounded all the while by Petra's mournful barks.

CHAPTER 10

THE BACKLIGHT FROM COUNTESS CLEO'S TABLET bounced off of her hoop earrings and reflected gold specks around the faculty room. Behind her were the VILE faculty—Coach Brunt, Dr. Saira Bellum, and Professor Maelstrom—standing around the screen.

"Have you conducted the public tours I advised?" Countess Cleo asked in a commanding tone.

A very round head nodded back at Countess Cleo. "My guides hosted three hundred visitors from the public today." Salvador de Burgos was video conferencing the VILE faculty from his secret study, flanked by his bodyguards. The bodyguards stared straight ahead and didn't look at the screen. If they thought it was unusual that their boss was video chatting with a covert band of thieves on an uncharted island, they didn't show it.

"That'll shake 'em off the scent!" Coach Brunt said encouragingly.

"Yes, yes," Dr. Bellum murmured.

"Was the public grateful for your generosity?" Professor Maelstrom asked with an arched eyebrow.

"*¡Sí, claro!*" de Burgos replied. "My staff received many compliments, and the local papers have all published articles about my magnanimity in allowing the public to enjoy my treasures while they mourn the loss of the recently discovered silver castle." Salvador de Burgos threw back his head and laughed.

"As I always say, a little good deed goes a long way to keep the investigations away!" Countess Cleo said merrily. She had in fact never said that before, but it was obvious how true it was: if the entirety of Spain was convinced that Salvador de Burgos was a generous old man who wanted to share his love of art with the people of Sevilla, then they would hardly suspect him of an evil crime.

"Now that I've shaken inquiring detectives, tell me, when will I receive *mi precioso león*?" He rubbed his hands together greedily.

"You'll receive your precious lion only for the agreed-upon price," Countess Cleo said sternly.

De Burgos waved his hand. "Cost isn't an issue. Once the silver lion is in my possession, you will have your fee."

Countess Cleo frowned. "I hope you don't plan to resell. I shall be *very* angry if I learn of the throne going for a higher price after what we have done."

De Burgos put his hand on his heart. "I would never sell such a treasure. Of that you can be sure. Once you have delivered the silver lion to me, I shall sit upon the Throne of Felipe!"

Professor Maelstrom interrupted, "I believe you *have* the Throne of Felipe, Salvador de Burgos. Was it not received at your residence this afternoon?"

A goofy smile spread across Salvador de Burgos's face. He turned the camera, giving the VILE faculty a view of the inside of his secret study, filled with priceless treasures as it was. In the corner stood the large refrigerator box. De Burgos looked at it as if it were a beloved child, then turned the camera back to himself with a satisfied smirk. "Now tell me, when will the missing inlays be delivered to me?"

With a haughty toss of her head, Countess Cleo replied, "The silver castle is already in VILE possession, as you know. I should inform you that the castle was *heavily* secured in the Archivo, and that only a skilled VILE operative would have been able to break through these defenses."

"And I'm very grateful," de Burgos said in a thoroughly unimpressed tone. "What I want to know is when the inlays will be in *my* possession."

"The same operative who secured the castle will search for the silver lion tonight."

Salvador de Burgos pouted. "You mean you don't know *where* the lion is now?"

Professor Maelstrom spoke very slowly, as if he were explaining something to a young child. "The lion has been missing for centuries. You cannot expect it to be found in an instant. We have hope that the lion is somewhere in the maze where the silver castle was found — but you must be patient while our operative searches the maze — it could be the work of a week! Then we will deliver the lion and the castle to you together."

Salvador de Burgos folded his hands. "I expect a delivery by dawn tomorrow."

Over the faculty's loud protestations, de Burgos closed his laptop, and the screen in the VILE faculty lounge went black.

CHAPTER 11

CARMEN DIDN'T THINK VERY HIGHLY of the Spanish police. She picked the lock of the AGI with a hairpin in fifteen seconds flat. Whatever additional security they had put in place before the silver castle was stolen, it was gone now. Carmen walked right into the dark archive, her red trench coat fully loaded with tools.

"No sign of guards, cameras, alarms, anything," she said into her earring. "It's like after the castle was stolen, they decided to give up."

"Hey, if VILE got that thing out of a locked glass case without breaking the lock or the glass at my archive, I'd give up too," Player said.

"No, you wouldn't."

"You have to hand it to them, it was impressive."

Carmen shook her head. "Don't give them any credit, Player. Evil isn't impressive, no matter how skilled the operative." She strode back toward the hallway with the trapdoor. It wasn't even roped off anymore. She kicked the left corner and the trapdoor sprung open. Carmen looked down. All she saw was stair after stair, then darkness. It was like climbing into a black hole. She took a deep breath and began her descent.

It was slow going, testing each step as she went, feeling for the stone walls on either side in the darkness. If she lost her footing, it would be a long way down.

Carmen counted steps. After the first hundred down, the walls on either side of the narrow stone stairs disappeared, replaced simply by open air. If she fell now, she would surely break her neck.

It grew cooler and more humid as she climbed lower, like the inside of an unusually deep cellar.

"You doing okay, Red?" Player asked softly.

"All clear," Carmen replied. "It's just one foot in front of the other right now." She was two hundred steps deep. She guesstimated she had a few more hundred to go.

"Let's recap today," Player said. "This Salvador de Burgos character sounds pretty fishy. Who has a hidden room in their *house?*"

"There was definitely something fishy about it," Carmen said. "But I can't figure out how exactly he fits into all of this. VILE is definitely behind the theft of the silver castle—no one else could have gotten it out of that glass case, and, anyway, we already knew they had taken the throne."

"Maybe he's their local host," Player said. "A kind of evil hospitality guy."

"I don't think that's a thing."

She could almost hear Player shrugging on the other end of the line.

"Maybe he's a kind of black-market salesman," Carmen said. "He might be helping VILE find rich art collectors. Only he didn't sound like he was lying when he said he would never sell the throne."

"You think that delivery really was the throne?"

"Had to be," Carmen said. "Why else put it in a secret room?"

"He has a reputation for being a bit of a spoiled glutton. Maybe he really just wanted a refrigerator in his private room—sure beats going down to the kitchen every time you're hungry," said Player.

"You think Salvador de Burgos makes his own sandwiches? I can guarantee you he has servants for that."

Player laughed. "I'm only joking about the refrigerator. I agree with you—he's up to something with that throne. I'll tell Zack and Ivy to patrol around de Burgos's mansion. Make sure he doesn't get up to anything funny while we're down here—"

"Player," Carmen interrupted. "I think I reached the bottom." She slid her foot as far out in front of her as she could, making sure it wasn't just some midway landing. But it wasn't. She was in the maze below the Archivo General de Indias, deep below the city of Sevilla, Spain.

Carmen found the nearest wall and inched along it, using her hands to feel for anything unusual on the surface of the wall, and sweeping a flashlight in every direction. The maze looked unremarkable. All around she saw only the same rough tan stone that all of Sevilla seemed to be built from. So far, there were no forks or unexpected turns. She followed what felt like an endless tunnel. Finally, she turned a sharp corner and was standing in front of the vault where the silver castle had been found.

It was unmistakable. Carmen supposed building the vault in a maze deep below the city was enough disguise, but she hadn't expected it to be so ostentatious. The door was layered with gold and silver, and over it was some kind of inscription. Carmen shone her flashlight at it.

PARA LA GLORIA DEL REY DE ESPAÑA,
LOS TESOROS DEL MERCADERO
JOAQUÍN REINOSO

"Red, fill me in—what do you see?"

Carmen translated in her head. As weird as it was to be grateful for anything VILE had done, it wasn't the first time she was glad to have had so many different nannies from around the world—Spanish was just one of the languages she could speak well. "There's an inscription above the entrance to the vault. It says, *For the glory of the king of Spain, the treasures of the merchant Joaquín Reinoso.*"

Player snorted. "Except he hid them well out of sight. Sounds like a good way to avoid the king's taxes."

Carmen tugged on the door. "He figured he was on the good list after getting the king that throne."

"Yeah, finding a chair that could fit a chin like that."

Player and Carmen were both laughing as she entered the vault. It was the size of a walk-in closet, and of course it had been emptied after the researcher had discovered it the week before. But Carmen could see the shelves that a short time before had held precious stones, gold, and silver. She scoured each shelf for any clues that had been left behind, but there was nothing there. She let herself out of the vault and closed the door behind her.

"Let's see what else this maze has hidden."

"It had better be a silver lion."

"And we had better be the first ones here."

"Speaking of which," said Player. "Any sign of our friends?"

"No," said Carmen, "but I can't imagine they haven't already searched this maze. When I talked to Salvador de Burgos, it became *pretty* clear that all three silver shapes together with the throne is the real prize. VILE might be two steps ahead of me for all I know—but I'm hoping there's something they overlooked down here, because I don't have any other leads."

Carmen reached into her pocket. Searching this maze was definitely a job for Red Drone, a tiny tool that could fly up to any door or wall, record videos and x-rays, and communicate with security systems. She loaded it up and let it fly around the maze a few feet ahead of her, x-raying the walls and sending the data back to Player's home computer.

"Nothing there," Player said. "Just rock in every direction."

"There's gotta be something somewhere." Carmen moved faster, and Red Drone sped up to keep pace with her. She came to a fork, made a split-second decision, and raced down the new tunnel.

"Red, do we have a plan to get you out of here later?" Player asked.

"One step ahead of you," Carmen replied. "We're doing this Hansel and Gretel style—with a little update." Behind her was a trail of children's glow sticks. Every few feet she reached into her pocket, grabbed a glow stick, cracked it to activate the light, and dropped it on her path. "The package said guaranteed to stay lit for eight hours. That should give us time."

"I like your style," Player said. "Plus, now we're ready for Halloween."

"Player, that was dad-joke level."

Player laughed. "Just trying to keep things light while you're six thousand feet under."

Carmen groaned.

"Wait! I see something!"

Carmen stopped in her tracks. Red Drone was buzzing in place. "Behind that wall?"

"Yeah," Player said. "Not much is coming in on my screen, but there's definitely something behind there. Can you look?"

Carmen shone her flashlight where Red Drone was hovering. It looked like an ordinary wall. Undeterred, Carmen walked forward and started pressing her palm down all around the area, hoping to find a lever or a button like the one that had let her into Salvador de Burgos's private study. But there was nothing.

"It's just a wall, I think," Carmen said.

"But there's something back there! Empty space, it's got to be some kind of secret hidey-hole!"

"Wait a second," Carmen said. "There's a turn just up ahead. I'm going to check it out." Dropping another glow stick as she went, Carmen rounded the corner. "There's a door here! I see it!"

It was completely unlike the entrance to the other vault. This was a stone door whose outline was only faintly visible. It blended into the wall the way the trapdoor had blended into the floor. The hinges were flat and rusty. There was no doorknob.

Carmen slid a thin knife into the crack between the door and the wall, until it met the latch. She pushed down, and the latch gave way. She stepped inside.

CHAPTER 12

NO ONE HAD BEEN INSIDE THIS VAULT for hundreds of years. It had the silent, hallowed feel of a place undisturbed by human affairs. Carmen tread slowly and quietly.

This space was the same size as the other vault, but it was modest. Carmen was standing on reddish dirt; the stone floor ended at the door. There were shelves like in the other room, but they were made of roughly chopped wood, each one uneven, warped, and full of knotholes.

Piles of papers were stacked on each shelf. The stacks of paper looked almost like parchment: thick and brown, and curling at the edges. A wax candle had melted onto one of the shelves, and Carmen shuddered, imagining what a fire could do in these underground tunnels.

For a long time, Carmen just stood and stared at the stacks of paper. Who had put them there? Why had they hidden these documents in particular? Had the merchant

Joaquín Reinoso known about this other vault, or was it built behind his back? Most of all, who was Carmen to disturb this untouched spot?

"Must be pretty important stuff, if someone took all the trouble to hide it," Player said, voicing Carmen's thoughts.

"Yeah, I guess so." Carmen turned left and right, letting the light from her flashlight shine over all the shelves. With steady hands, she lifted a stack of papers off the shelf farthest to the left. She would work counterclockwise around the vault. After all, she had almost eight hours left.

At first, it was hard to make any sense of the papers. They were written in Spanish, in an old and unusual script. Carmen had never learned much cursive, and even if she had, the writer's handwriting was completely unruly. But after a few minutes of squinting and turning the paper in different directions, things started to make sense to Carmen: she caught words like *plata* (silver) and *artesanía* (handicrafts), and soon she was reading entire sentences.

The first stack of papers wasn't very interesting. They were written by a master silversmith by the name of León Mondragón. He described different orders he had filled, for objects like candlesticks, vases, and tableaus for church altars. But a few stacks of papers in, Carmen realized that León Mondragón was more interesting than his accounts originally led on. He was born in 1590 in the city of Potosí, Bolivia—which, Carmen realized, perking up, was where the silver shapes had first been made! He described the city so well it was as if Carmen was really there herself. Potosí, according to León Mondragón, was full of little squares and tiny churches, and markets selling everything you could imagine. There were women selling chicha, which was a type of beer made from corn—*doesn't sound that tasty,* Carmen thought—concoctions to cure altitude sickness—*could have used that in Ecuador*—and different breads and cloths. People in Potosí dressed well. In fact, most of them sounded a little vain, according to Mondragón's words.

A creek that people called "La Ribera" ran through the city, and it powered the mills that ground the ore, which was like a kind of rock filled with pieces of silver. Then workers separated the crushed-up rock from the silver.

At first, Carmen thought making silver was kind of fun—the way Mondragón described the rock turning into silver sounded a little bit like one of those mica-cleaning machines that Coach Brunt had gotten her as a kid. But the more she read, the more she realized that silver mining was actually horrible. The Spanish conquerors wouldn't go into the mines themselves, because it was dark, back-breaking, and dangerous down there. Instead they forced Indigenous people (people who were native to the Andes) to go mining for them. The workers had to bring their own tools, and some of those tools were expensive—leather bags to carry up the ore, and candles, which were really valuable back then, to illuminate the dark mines. The workers counted on their kids and wives to bring them food, because it's not like the Spanish would feed them. Sometimes, Indigenous miners could make good money, because they got to take home some of what they had mined. But other times, they made barely anything—and they were still forced to work.

Carmen balled her fists in anger, thinking, *No one should have to work in those conditions.* She read on and learned that León Mondragón was a mestizo, which meant he was half Indigenous, half Spanish. His mother was Lupaca (an Indigenous group in the Andes) and had spoken to León in a language called Aymara. The Lupaca people in Potosí lived a little upland of La Ribera, near the mine—which people in Potosí called either the "Cerro Rico" (Rich Hill) or the "Cerro Rojo" (Red Hill), because from far away, the dirt made it look reddish. Mondragón's mother's people had not been well off, but they had been lucky to avoid mine work and hone their talents as artisans. It was from his mother that León Mondragón had gotten his skill and interest in art and crafting. Mondragón's father was a poor Spaniard who had come to Potosí hoping to make his fortune—and failed spectacularly. Mondragón did not have a charmed childhood, but he was grateful that his father had secured him an apprenticeship with a silversmith at a young age, and he fell in love with the craft of silver working.

León Mondragón must have written every day of his life, because he had chronicled everything: he wrote about the teams of llamas and mules that carried supplies from the countryside, about the vicuñas and the vizcachas, the large and small animals that lived in the highlands just outside the city, and about the shocking-pink flamingos that flocked to shallow pools that formed nearby.

León loved living way up in the mountains, but he often wondered about life outside of Potosí. Even though Potosí held many mestizos like him, León was never quite sure whether he really belonged more with his Lupaca family or with his Spanish family. He thought he might like to travel, to visit Spain and see with his own eyes the many works of silver that he and other artisans in Potosí had made for wealthy Spaniards. There was a line in León's writing that caught Carmen's attention. He talked about being half Spanish but not having seen Spain with his own eyes, and how hard it was to be both Spanish and Lupaca when he knew what the Spaniards were doing to so many of his people in the mines.

He's just like Milly, Carmen thought. *He belongs to two places at once.*

Finally, León de Mondragón started writing about the Throne of Felipe. Carmen found a diagram of the throne's base, which was sent to León by a secretary of the merchant Joaquín Reinoso. The diagram showed exactly where the inlays would go, and what size and shape they had to be. León would have to match the dimensions given precisely, so that when the inlays were sent to Spain, they would fit in the spots that the throne's carpenter had carved out for them. If León was off by so much as a hair, the inlays wouldn't fit, and the throne would be unadorned.

León described how hard he worked on the inlays, how he tried to make the feather at the end of the silver arrow seem real, and how he wanted the castle to seem three-dimensional. When he described the lion, Carmen felt a thrill going up and down her spine. León talked about carving the lion midroar, how he wanted the viewer to *feel* the lion's hot breath and the reverberations of his powerful roar. That's how lifelike he wanted his carving to be.

León was clearly proud of his work, but there was also a sadness to his writing. He showed his neighbors and friends his work when it was finished, but all too soon the inlays had to be packed up to make the long journey to Spain. To León, that didn't feel fair. Indigenous people had mined and ground the ore, had refined it into silver, and he had shaped it into beautiful designs. But the only people who would get to enjoy this work were those in Spain—powerful people, who knew the king himself. León wished the inlays could have stayed in Potosí for the people of the city to enjoy them.

And yet—León was so conflicted—he said it was like sending a message in a bottle, knowing his work would cross an ocean he had never crossed and leave a city he had never left. Maybe someone would see his work and be inspired to make their own art. Maybe someone would be moved by his skill. He imagined that if even one person in Spain felt a connection to his work, León wouldn't feel isolated on his mountain anymore. His art would be like a conversation across the distance of the ocean.

Carmen stopped reading. León's words now reminded her of someone else: herself. She understood exactly what León meant by wanting a connection to someone outside his mountain, wanting to know that someone out there understood him. She remembered when she was living on Vile Island and Player figured out how to hack into the VILE network and call her cellphone. He didn't know who he was calling—he was just hacking for fun. At first, Carmen wasn't sure whether to trust Player. But before long, her curiosity got the better of her. Player knew what life was like off the island, and Carmen had never been anywhere but the island—well, not since she had been found as a baby, which she didn't remember anyway.

"Red?" said Player, into her earring. "What's the latest?"

Carmen smiled. She remembered the first time Player had used her nickname—when they video chatted right after she ran away from Vile Island. He'd asked her if she was okay, and called her Red, because of the fedora she'd swiped from Cookie Booker as she made her escape.

"Everything's fine," Carmen said. "Something about León—he was the artisan who made the silver inlays, I've been reading his writing—he reminds me of myself."

"How so, Red?"

"Because he wanted a connection to the world outside his mountain. Like I wanted a connection to life outside Vile Island. When you hacked into my cellphone, I finally got that—talking to you was like getting a message in a bottle. I realized that there was a whole *universe* out there."

"I can understand that," Player said. "Feeling alone and wishing there was someone out there you could talk to." He sighed heavily, and Carmen got the feeling there was something he wasn't telling her—something he *wanted* to tell her but couldn't find the words.

"Player, how did you get into white-hat hacking, anyway?" Carmen blurted out.

It was a question he always seemed to avoid, and Carmen hadn't asked it for many months, not since those first few days after she had left Vile Island. She had asked back then because she had been surprised the first time she video chatted with him: his bedroom was like his voice, inviting and casual, with piles of electronics, baseball hats that never seemed to get worn, and a mini basketball hoop hooked over the door. But she had been expecting some kind of hacker headquarters and wanted to know how Player had gotten so good at hacking, and why he worked from his bedroom. But Player didn't seem to like the question, and Carmen was reluctant to pry. Yet sometimes she thought he might like to tell her, if she caught him at the right moment.

"Is this really the time, Red?

Carmen shrugged. "I have almost eight hours, remember?"

"Six now."

"That's a long time. Try me."

She listened closely to the silence on the other end of her comm-link earring.

Player sighed again. "I was looking for my dad," he mumbled. "He left a few years ago. He and my mom had been fighting, but I never expected he'd just disappear— and I had no idea where he had gone. I thought if I could just, you know, poke around some of his accounts—"

"And did you? Find him?" Carmen asked, interrupting him.

"I'm good at this, Red. It wasn't that hard. A little

tinkering with home security cameras, changing some account numbers—"

"Player! You changed your *dad's* account numbers?"

"Like I said, the guy ran out on me—and weren't you, let's see if I remember, an international *criminal?*"

"Yeah, but I saw the error in my ways."

"So did I!" Player said. "I found my dad, but then I realized my mom and I were just fine—we didn't need all the fighting, honestly."

Carmen felt terrible. Player might have a jovial, lighthearted tone, but if he had wanted to find his dad so badly—it couldn't have been easy.

"But by then I was already in the habit, you know? I realized you could find people online. And I found you!"

It took Carmen a little while to process what Player was saying. "So . . . you get it."

"Get what?" Player was breathing heavily, as if he had just gone running, but Carmen recognized the symptoms. It was the stress of reliving a difficult time. She always felt her heart racing when she remembered her time on Vile Island.

"You get what it's like to want to find someone."

"I get what it's like to be abandoned, if that's what you mean. You weren't the only one, Red."

"I'm sorry, Player," Carmen said softly. She wished she could think of something else to say, of a way to explain to him that he was the one holding the other end of her rope, and that she was grateful.

"Hey, it's okay. My mom got remarried and my step-dad is a great guy, so things are pretty good now. And hacking is like — what did you call it? A message in a bottle. I get to talk to you, and Zack and Ivy. It might be just me alone here in my room, but when I'm hacking — "

"It's like you've got your best friend's voice in your comm-link earring?"

"I mean I would never wear one of those, Red. But yeah, it's like that," Player said gruffly.

Carmen smiled ruefully. A silversmith in the Andes Mountains, an international criminal on an uncharted island, a guy in his bedroom missing his dad — they all had more in common than anyone could have guessed. And Carmen was grateful that Player had hacked into her cellphone, and that she had replied, like a shipwrecked sailor sending out a message in a bottle. A message that said: *Hey, world, I exist. My name is Carmen Sandiego, and here I come.*

CHAPTER 13

R ED?" PLAYER ASKED. "Maybe we should get back to the caper?"

Carmen shook herself. "Right, yes. We should."

"Does the silversmith give any clues about the silver lion?"

Not about where the lion was hidden, Carmen thought. She could vividly imagine the lion's lifelike roar from León Mondragón's description, but she had to admit she was no closer to knowing where it was hidden than she had been when she found the vault. She looked around, almost as if expecting the lion to be sitting there on a stack of papers. It would be a pretty strange thing to use as a paperweight.

"Player," Carmen said slowly. "There's one more thing." It was hard to express what she was thinking. Her neck and face felt warm, and she was vaguely glad that Player couldn't see her. "I never thanked you. Not really."

"Thanked me for what? For booking your plane tickets and using my sweet hacking skills?"

"No, not for that," Carmen said. "I mean, *thanks* for all that, of course. I meant for talking to me on Vile Island. For the messages in bottles, like we were saying. You were the only person who didn't think I was destined for great evil or whatever twisted future Professor Maelstrom and the rest of them had in mind."

"Aw, thanks, Red," Player said. "You're good to talk to yourself, you know. It can get" — Player coughed loudly, as if the words choked him — "pretty quiet around here without a caper on."

Carmen smiled. She and Player were lucky to have found one another. She stood up, dusted herself off, and went back over to the shelves. She needed to get serious about finding the silver lion.

"León Mondragón must have come to Spain eventually, because he created this vault."

"Right," Player agreed.

"But for all he wrote about wondering about the world outside Potosí, there doesn't seem to be any sign of what he actually *did* on his trip to Spain."

"Leave a letter explaining the whereabouts of the silver lion in the vault?" Player said hopefully.

"That would be ideal." Carmen laughed. But Player

was right—there had to be some kind of clue among these papers—otherwise why would Mondragón have gone through the trouble of creating this hiding spot, especially when it sounded like coming to Spain had been a bucket-list trip for him. If there weren't some kind of secret involved, he would have had better things to do than creep around underground, hiding documents.

There were three stacks of papers left. Carmen rifled through the first set and groaned when she realized that it was nothing but charts with long strings of numbers—León Mondragón's billing and accounts. She turned to the second stack of papers, and her heart sank as she flipped through even more charts and numbers. She wondered whether there could be some kind of code or clue hidden in the numbers—but that kind of code would take hours, if not days, to decipher. Carmen considered stealing the papers so she could analyze them for clues. There just *had* to be something worth finding in this vault. A person who had nothing to hide didn't just build a secret vault deep below Sevilla for no reason.

Sighing, Carmen flipped through the last stack of papers. Charts, numbers, more charts, more numbers.

That was it. She had read every stack of paper in this entire vault. Clearly, León Mondragón—whenever it was he had come to Spain—had just built this hidey-hole for absolutely no reason. It's not like anyone was going to steal his old account papers. Carmen sighed and slumped against the wall.

She hit a stone that jutted out a few centimeters, and some sand and tiny pebbles drifted down the wall.

"Ow," Carmen complained aloud, rubbing her shoulder.

"What's up?" Player said. "Did you trip or something?"

"Wait a second!" Carmen said, straightening up. The sand and pebbles had fallen on the last stack of papers, which Carmen had been too frustrated to put back properly. A few sheets off the top floated down to the dirt floor. One of them had actual writing on it.

"What is it?" Player asked.

Carmen grabbed the paper off the ground. "Give me a minute," she told Player.

The paper had a detailed description of how León Mondragón had made the lion's fur, which, based on what was written here, was probably as detailed and lifelike as the feather on the silver arrow. Even though she'd gotten much more comfortable with León's handwriting, she still had to read slowly to decipher his loopy script. But even after she had read every detail about the tools he had used and the number of hours it had taken him to make the silver lion, there was nothing about *where* the lion could be found. Carmen was about ready to bang her head against the wall.

There were some scribbles on the bottom of the document, as if León had been testing his ink or something like that. He clearly was the sort of person who used a ruler, because each sheet of paper had a perfect one-inch margin all around. The scribbles were in the bottom margin, and Carmen was sort of surprised that León would do something that messy in the margins he had so neatly created—it wasn't like he could have used a computer back in the 1600s—but Carmen was so frustrated from not finding anything that she tossed the paper back onto the ground.

"Nothing, Player. There's nothing here. Total red herring. We're no closer to the silver lion than we were a few hours ago, and VILE is probably onto another lead."

"What were you looking at?" Player asked. "You seemed pretty excited."

"Just another document about how León Mondragón worked *so hard* to make the silver lion and the fur was *so lifelike* and no one understands the *artistry* that goes into it," Carmen complained.

Player snorted. "I thought we liked León Mondragón?"

In reality, Carmen had started to think of León as a friend. He loved silversmithing the way Carmen loved solving crimes, and she felt like he understood what it had been like for Carmen, growing up completely cut off from the outside world on Vile Island. But she did *not* like dead ends.

"There was nothing interesting on the document?" Player asked. "Nothing unusual?"

"Just some squiggles."

"Squiggles? Well, let's analyze them! Maybe they're a kind of special writing code."

"Worth a try," Carmen said. She snapped a scan of the squiggles and sent it over to Player.

She waited, while hearing Player click things on his computer.

"They do look like squiggles," Player admitted. "But I'm going to run these through an advanced character recognition program I made and see if anything comes up."

Carmen paced around while Player ran the photo through his software.

"Red! I found something!"

Carmen stopped in place. "What did you find?"

"These are definitely letters. Look at your phone, I just sent it back to you."

Her phone was buried deep in her coat—it wasn't something she usually used in the middle of a caper—so Carmen fished it out. She unlocked it and looked at the document Player had just sent over. It was the squiggles superimposed with typed letters. Player's program had figured out what the squiggles said!

"It's in Spanish," Carmen said.

"No kidding."

"Give me a minute to translate." Carmen said the words aloud as she read. *Fascinaba — entender — castillo — león —*

"I think," Carmen said slowly. That it means something like this. She read aloud to Player:

> *Only someone who cared about my story would seek out such a humble hidey-hole and read these papers. Perhaps that someone would understand — the rich merchant may keep among his treasures the silver castle, but he has not had the last word. The silver lion, they ask? Don't bother looking, it vanished into thin air.*

"You have *got* to be kidding me," Player said — and Carmen couldn't agree more.

CHAPTER 14

NEITHER PLAYER NOR CARMEN could think of anything to say. It had been a long search, only to come up empty.

Carmen was gathering herself to leave when a sound caught her attention. It was quiet at first, and far away. Some kind of ringing, buzzing noise. Carmen flattened herself against the wall of the vault, just to the right of the door. She was using an important trick from VILE Academy—this way, she would be hidden if the door was to swing open. She clutched the squiggle document in one hand and crossed her fingers with the other that the noise would move away. But the sound only grew closer, and the closer it came, the more Carmen recognized it as humming. A sweet, childlike tune.

There was only one person Carmen knew who would hum like that in an underground maze.

The door clicked open, and Carmen held her breath.

Through the crack in the hinges of the door, Carmen watched as Paperstar surveyed the stacks of papers and picked up a document to read. Carmen personally thought the VILE operatives should have to read all of León Mondragón's writing so they would understand how much work had gone into the throne they had so cruelly stolen, but if Paperstar spent as much time reading as Carmen had, it would be difficult to sneak out unnoticed. Carmen hoped she would move quickly.

Now Paperstar was dragging her fingers along the shelves. She picked up one of the charts, fingered the heavy paper, and in an instant folded it into a weapon, which she slipped into her pocket. Carmen tensed. She might have been frustrated that León Mondragón didn't leave any clues, but she still thought his words were important. She thought it mattered how hard he worked on his craft, and how angry he was about how the mine owners treated Indigenous people. She didn't want to see his words turn into nothing but tools for Paperstar's evil rampages, likely to end up in a gutter—or worse, slicing someone open.

Then suddenly, Paperstar lunged for something. Carmen's jaw dropped.

She had left her cellphone on the ground. Unlocked.

With the image of the squiggles and the typed words still open.

Please don't speak Spanish, Carmen thought.

"Interesting," Paperstar said aloud in her singsong voice. "That must mean my *little* friend is around here somewhere." She slipped the phone into her pocket.

This was not the time for hiding. "Player," Carmen hissed. "Wipe my phone's memory! Now!"

She jumped out from behind the door, slamming it shut. "What do you want, Paperstar?"

Paperstar shrugged. "Well, I already have your phone." She held it up, smiling sweetly. Carmen could still see the photo Player had sent on the screen.

"I'm working, Red!" Player said frantically into her earring. "There's a lot of data on that phone — it'll take a few minutes to back up and clear!"

Carmen had no choice but to distract Paperstar. "So," she said, hoping to get Paperstar talking. "I see you found my hiding place."

Paperstar waved a glow stick in front of Carmen's face. "You didn't exactly make it hard. Amateur hour — didn't even cover up your tracks."

Carmen laughed. "I think my tracks are going to come in pretty useful when I'm trying to find our way out of here."

"Oh, you're not leaving anytime soon!" Paperstar remarked cheerfully. She lunged for the door and locked it. "Tell me everything you know about the silver lion."

Carmen almost breathed a sigh of relief. However much time she had wasted reading León Mondragón's papers, at least VILE hadn't gotten the silver lion in the meantime. Then she had an idea. She crossed her arms.

"What do you want to know?"

"Where it is and how I get it from you," Paperstar growled.

Carmen balled up the document in her hand—*sorry, León,* she said to herself—and opened up her coat, giving Paperstar a one-second glimpse at the tools inside. "Too bad I can't help you. The silver lion has been moved to a secure location."

Paperstar's eyes narrowed. "And you're going to tell me where that secure location is, *right?*"

"Now, why would I do a thing like that?"

"Because if you don't—" Paperstar lunged toward Carmen, who ducked and rolled to the other end of the vault. She jumped up and paced around Paperstar, ready to pounce. Eyes locked, the two made a circle. Carmen's phone glowed in Paperstar's hand, still clearly unlocked and loaded with Carmen's information. Carmen sprung toward Paperstar, who tossed the phone up and caught it as Carmen fell past her.

"Here's a deal. Tell me where the silver lion is, and you get back your phone. Don't tell me and — hooray! I'll have a new toy all to myself."

"As if I would tell you," Carmen said, trying to buy time. "But here's the thing, Paperstar. There's a clue about the silver lion. You can find it all by yourself if you look. You don't need me at all."

"And what is that?" Paperstar crossed her arms.

"In those papers." Carmen nodded toward the shelves. "That's where the clues are. Sit down and read those, and you'll know everything I know about the silver lion."

Paperstar turned for just a second and Carmen made another desperate grab for her phone, but Paperstar yanked it away. In that moment Carmen saw her phone flash with these words:

⚠️ **MEMORY WIPED**
RETURNED TO FACTORY SETTINGS

Carmen breathed a sigh of relief. "Actually," she said cheerfully, "I never knew anything about the silver lion. I don't have it at a secure location." If Paperstar didn't have her phone's memory, Carmen sure didn't need to keep her here talking. "See ya!" Carmen jumped, flipped the lock, and kicked open the door. She tore down the maze, picking up glow sticks as she ran. This time, she would definitely be covering her tracks.

Unfortunately, Paperstar was close behind, following Carmen's footsteps instead of the glow sticks. Carmen looked up, as if a way to shake Paperstar would somehow appear out of nowhere, but the narrow maze didn't give her many options. All she could do was run, staying a step ahead of Paperstar.

They reached the stairs and Carmen took off, desperate to reach the trapdoor and not be overtaken. Carmen climbed and climbed. A square of reddish light appeared above her, and she almost cheered. It was the Archivo, illuminated that night only by the glow of an emergency exit sign. Carmen threw herself upward, wriggled through the trapdoor, and shut it behind her as quickly as she could. A closed door wouldn't stop Paperstar for long, but it would buy her a few minutes.

She raced out of the museum and onto the street. The plaza was softly lit by streetlamps, and a couple was kissing on a bench. Carmen picked a direction and dashed off just as the museum door swung open and shut behind her—Paperstar was on the chase again.

The night was warm and breezy, and Carmen noticed a tall tower gracing the skyline of Sevilla. "Player," she asked breathlessly. "What's that tower thing?"

Player was only too glad to play tour guide, even in the

middle of a chase. "That would be La Giralda, Red. It's one of Sevilla's most well-known monuments. When this part of Spain was ruled by Islamic people, it was a minaret — then later, when Christian rulers took over, they used the same structure as a bell tower for the cathedral."

Carmen was impressed. It was like an interfaith Muslim-Christian monument rolled all into one. "Looks like it'll make a good Paperstar escape plan," she told Player. "Scaling the tower should slow down those darts of hers."

Luckily, La Giralda had lots of uneven spots that made good footholds for climbing, and Carmen had a head start on Paperstar. She was several stories up before she heard Paperstar's humming creeping up below her. She looked down — it was lucky Carmen wasn't afraid of heights — and Paperstar growled at her like an angry dog. Carmen kept climbing, but Paperstar was on her tail.

Suddenly Carmen felt a sharp tugging at her ankle, and she knew Paperstar had reached her. She shook her ankle loose, hoping to knock down Paperstar in the process — maybe climbing up this high hadn't been such a great idea after all, but it was too late now. There was a very narrow balcony at the top of the tower, and Carmen scrambled onto the rail, balancing precariously. She wasn't afraid; heights were a hazard of her job. She just hoped Paperstar couldn't throw and balance at the same time. Below, the city of Sevilla twinkled, and the water of the Guadalquivir River looked black and shimmery, slinking like a snake toward the coast.

Unfortunately, Paperstar *could* throw and balance at the same time, and now Carmen was ducking and jumping out of the way, all while balancing on a two-inch strip of rail. She fished in her coat for something to throw back at Paperstar when her fingers grazed a piece of paper, shoved into her pocket. She pulled it out and looked at it.

Paperstar saw her look. "Give me that!" she shrieked. Five paper darts assailed Carmen, who stepped backwards on the rail like a tightrope walker to get out of their way in time. "I hate to break it to you, Black Sheep, but I'm not leaving until you tell me where you've got that silver lion!"

Carmen muttered into her comm-link earring as she backwards-balance-walked around La Giralda, "Talk about a white lie that got out of hand!"

"She really thinks you know where the silver lion is, huh?" Player said.

"Not a good time to talk!" Carmen replied, jumping backwards and grabbing the rail with her left hand just in time. She swung herself around and jumped back up.

Meanwhile, Paperstar was clutching the rail with all fours like a possum and scooting toward Carmen.

"Um," Carmen said. This was a new tactic.

"That paper is mine!" Paperstar said. "You're obviously hiding the location; I can see the writing from here!"

Something clicked. Carmen glanced down at the crumpled paper. She smoothed it out. *Paperstar* thought the paper contained an important clue. It *did* contain a clue, but all the clue told them was that the silver lion was gone, probably lost forever. It didn't do Carmen any good to keep hanging on to it, as much as she liked having a little piece of her long-gone-almost-friend León Mondragón in her pocket.

"Hey, Paperstar," Carmen said casually. "You want this?" She waved the document in the air.

Paperstar straightened up, inches from Carmen.

"Let's make a trade. *You* tell me where VILE has the stolen silver castle, and *I'll* give this clue to you."

"Not a chance."

"How about you tell me where VILE is keeping its headquarters in Sevilla?"

"Are you kidding me?" Paperstar's eyes didn't leave the document clutched in Carmen's hand. Carmen kept moving her body and the paper around, trying to keep Paperstar's focus.

"But you want to show your other VILE friends this clue, don't you, Paperstar?"

"I *will* show them that clue!" Paperstar shouted, pouncing toward Carmen.

That was all Carmen needed to hear. Paperstar grabbed the document from her. While Paperstar roared triumphantly, Carmen lost her footing, slipped, and tumbled off the tower.

CHAPTER 15

THE NIGHT OWLS IN SEVILLA paid no attention to a figure that hummed and skipped through the streets. Paperstar, confident that Black Sheep had been crushed falling from the top of La Giralda, was on her way toward VILE headquarters, proudly holding the document she had snatched from Carmen. In her own not-so-humble opinion, this was her best feat yet—stealing an important clue from Black Sheep while balanced high in the air. She would be showered with praise and given all the best assignments for years to come. Paperstar beamed at the paper in front of her. She didn't know what it meant, and of course she thought making weapons was a much better use of paper than writing things on it, but she knew the VILE faculty would be pleased. Maybe she'd go back to that vault later and get some of the extra paper for her darts. This old stuff was quality—heavy and thick.

A hundred feet above, Carmen Sandiego hung from a protrusion on the side of La Giralda, watching Paperstar's progress. When Paperstar started to fade from sight, Carmen fastened her grappling hook to a crevice and propelled down the side of the tower. She reached the plaza below, gathered up her grappling hook, and followed the street Paperstar had taken. She knew Paperstar would be bringing the useless document to VILE's hideout in Sevilla, where it would be scanned and sent to the faculty. This was Carmen's one shot to find out where the VILE operatives were hiding—and where they were keeping the silver castle.

She caught up with Paperstar and shrank into the shadows, staying far enough away that Paperstar never suspected her—and neither did any passerby. Paperstar went onto smaller and narrower streets, turning every few feet. No one seemed to be awake in this part of town; the buildings on either side were dark, and their balconies were shuttered. Decorative tiles on the sides of corner buildings marked the street names, and Carmen caught whiffs of orange blossoms. If she hadn't been in the middle of a chase, she might have enjoyed a night walk through Sevilla.

Now Paperstar skipped through an archway that opened up onto a modern plaza, crowded with parked motorcycles, sidewalk cafés, and little markets advertising different types of soda and candy in their windows.

Carmen followed Paperstar across the empty plaza, then reached a busy road. Even at this hour, cars were zooming past. Carmen waited, and as soon as the light changed, she skulked after Paperstar, crossing multiple lanes of cars. Now Paperstar crossed a patch of grass and turned onto a quiet pedestrian boulevard. During the day the path was probably full of bikers and joggers and tourists, but at this hour it was nearly deserted.

"I'm tracking your location, Red—I think she's leading you to the river!"

Sure enough, the boulevard curved around, and soon they were walking along the bank of a wide river.

"The Guadalquivir River flows from the Atlantic Ocean into Sevilla," Player explained. "It's important for Spanish history because ships used to come to and from America using that river."

Interesting, Carmen thought.

"I wonder where VILE would hide around there— it's mostly apartment buildings. You think they rented a place?"

That sounded all too law-abiding for VILE, but one way or another, Carmen would find out where they were hiding. She hadn't let Paperstar out of her sight.

A breeze rose from the river, and the current carried along an occasional soda can or large branch. Once, a barge sailed by, blowing its horn as it reached a curve.

Ahead, a tower loomed over the boulevard. It was short and squat—the exact opposite of La Giralda— and Carmen guessed it was no more than three stories tall. It wasn't round or square like most towers Carmen had seen around the world. Instead, this tower had many flat sides—Carmen couldn't count how many from where she was standing. It looked like some kind of strange sentry box in a military fortress. From the center a smaller tower rose like the second layer of a cake, and the roof was topped by a gold spire.

"What's the building ahead of me?" Carmen asked quietly.

Player took a second to reply. "La Torre del Oro," he said finally. "It was built in the thirteenth century—that's even older than the Throne of Felipe—to guard the river. Hey, this is cool—the Torre del Oro is a *dodecagon*—it has twelve different sides."

Carmen stopped in place. Paperstar was strolling toward the tower, even though it was clearly closed at night. She pulled something out of her pocket, hovered it on the side of the tower, and a door sprang open. Paperstar disappeared into the Torre del Oro.

"Player," Carmen said. "I've found VILE's hideout. They're in the Torre del Oro. And I'm going to need backup."

CHAPTER 16

VILE ISLAND WAS FULL of excitement. Every student and faculty member knew by now that Paperstar had successfully stolen a clue from Carmen Sandiego, and that the clue would lead them to the missing silver lion. Countess Cleo's classes that week had focused exclusively on the Throne of Felipe, and there wasn't anyone left on the island who didn't know that the mahogany carving of the throne was a work of art and that the silver inlays had been made by an expert artisan in the city of Potosí. Most of all, Countess Cleo had emphasized how much *money* VILE was about to make. Countess Cleo made sure everyone knew that life on Vile Island would now be financed by *her* master plot to steal the Throne of Felipe, reunite it with its silver inlays, and sell it to the billionaire Salvador de Burgos.

Paperstar, Le Chèvre, and El Topo were on site in Sevilla, applying high-tech scanning to the document so it could be sent back to Vile Island for analysis. Paperstar admitted freely that she didn't read Spanish, and El Topo admitted just as freely that he couldn't read a word of the handwriting, whatever language it was. So Countess Cleo and the VILE faculty were all gathered around Dr. Saira Bellum's multiscreened computer, eager to crack the clue.

When the image first arrived, the VILE faculty were delighted. Coach Brunt put two fingers in her mouth and whistled, Dr. Saira Bellum rubbed her hands together greedily, Countess Cleo clapped daintily, and a slow grin spread across Professor Maelstrom's face.

Dr. Bellum immediately started copying the image onto each of her different screens, instructing one to blow up the image, another to run character-recognition technology, and a third to automatically translate. When the translation was complete, everyone leaned in and squinted.

Countess Cleo was the first to break the silence. "The silversmith describes the detailed fur on the silver lion's back. Of course. That detail is what makes this piece so valuable."

Coach Brunt chuckled. "That detail, honeybee, is what makes this piece of paper *useless*."

Professor Maelstrom grunted with disgust. Meanwhile, Dr. Bellum clicked through to the other screens. She was undeterred by the boring writing on the document. Why would the silversmith think anyone would care about his artistic process? She cared where the money was. She zoomed out from the original image they had received from the operatives in the field, trying to get a sense of the document. Perhaps there was something written with invisible ink, or a seal that could only be read with a black light. Dr. Bellum was experienced with many types of codes and could surely crack this one.

"But wait!" Dr. Bellum exclaimed. "There's more!" She flipped her short hair off to the side.

"That there?" Coach Brunt asked. "That's all hat and no cattle, if you ask me."

"One never knows." Dr. Bellum clicked around more and applied the character-recognition software to the squiggles. Within seconds, typed words appeared above the squiggles. She copied and pasted and ran them through her translation program.

This time, no one said anything. Countess Cleo did not break the silence. In fact, Countess Cleo said, "Oh!" and fainted.

"Bless her heart!" Coach Brunt exclaimed. "She's passed out completely. The shock of it, poor lamb."

Dr. Bellum didn't look away from the screen. "Vanished into thin air?" she said to herself. "How could silver vanish into thin air?"

Professor Maelstrom shouted for a student, who promptly brought a towel and cold drink for Countess Cleo. Coach Brunt fanned her face.

By the time Countess Cleo sat up, Dr. Bellum had saved the clue and put it away. No point reliving the trauma. Countess Cleo had been so certain that the silver lion would be a cinch to find—likely hidden just a few feet away from the silver castle in the same vault. Apparently, she had been very, *very* wrong.

Countess Cleo touched her hair and adjusted her earrings. She stood and dusted herself off, trying to look dignified. Elegant women like her should not be lying on the floor. She settled herself onto a chair and faced her colleagues. "Well, then," she announced, "I shall discuss this with Salvador de Burgos. After all, if the silver lion doesn't *exist*, it's not as if we failed to find it for him."

"Not sure he'll see it that way, sweetums," Coach Brunt said.

Countess Cleo glared at Coach Brunt. "He will accept the symbolic value of having every *existing* silver inlay, plus the throne, in his possession. VILE operatives have successfully broken into not one but *two* high-security locations to accomplish this heist on his behalf and he will pay for it!" Countess Cleo cleared her voice. It had gotten high-pitched and sounded panicky for a moment there, not at all aristocratic.

Coach Brunt glanced at her watch. "We've got Paper-star, Le Chèvre, and El Topo all waiting for instructions. What's it to be?"

Professor Maelstrom stayed silent, his face cold. Dr. Bellum was already checking something else on one of her many screens. It was Countess Cleo's call.

"We call Paperstar. It is time to reunite the silver castle with the Throne of Felipe. *Tonight.*"

CHAPTER 17

CARMEN SURVEYED THE PERIMETER of the Torre del Oro. She wasn't sure what kind of security VILE had installed, but Paperstar had clearly used some kind of electronic card to get in. Carmen found the sensor by the door. She dug in her trench coat and pulled out a credit card. She tapped it to the sensor, which flashed back red. Carmen shrugged. It was worth a try.

She examined the lock and grabbed a hairpin from her coat, then snaked the hairpin into the old-fashioned keyhole, jiggling the lock pins. To her surprise, the lock loosened right away. She shook her head. Leave it to VILE to install an electronic system on an eight-hundred-year-old lock.

Carmen held the door and closed it softly behind her. She cocked her head to the side and listened, but heard nothing.

The ground floor of the tower was taken up by a

museum of naval history. There were models of boats and seafaring instruments in glass cases, along with paintings of monarchs on the wall. Carmen was relieved to see that these monarchs had a little less chin than the Felipes.

Carmen examined a banner that hung from the ceiling—red and yellow, which were the colors of the Spanish flag, with a design of castles and lions stitched onto it. She remembered what Salvador de Burgos had said about how castles and lions represented the two different kingdoms that had come together and conquered the rest of the country—*Castillo* (castle) and *León* (lion).

Carmen stopped in place. *León.* It occurred to her for the first time that the silver lion had maybe meant more to León Mondragón than the other inlays because it represented his name. Maybe making it had been like stamping his signature: one of a kind. It must have killed León to give the lion away to a long-chinned monarch thousands of miles away.

Footsteps sounded above, and Carmen circled the ground floor. She found a metal door and tugged it open. Inside was a narrow staircase with hazard tape on the edge of each step. Tiptoeing for silence, Carmen climbed the stairs. After two stories, there was a landing, and she found another door, with another staircase. This one was far narrower than the first—it was surely leading into the second tower, the one that was like the top of a layer cake.

At the end of the stairwell was a final door. Carmen put her ear against it and listened closely.

It took a moment for her ears to adjust, but then Carmen was able to pick up snippets of conversation. There was intermittent humming, so surely Paperstar was inside. She caught a few words.

"Yes, the castle." It was Le Chèvre speaking, and it sounded like he was on the phone with someone. "It'll be there before dawn — yes, *well* before dawn."

Where would it be before dawn? Carmen pressed her ear closer to the door and strained to hear.

"You will alert his body men, yes?"

"And tell him to put away that annoying dog," El Topo complained.

Carmen pulled back from the door. If they were trying to get there before dawn — Carmen sped down the narrow staircase, yanked open the door on the first landing, and closed it behind her.

"Player," she said into her earring. "Tell Zack and Ivy to be on high alert! I'll meet them at Salvador de Burgos's as soon as I can!"

Carmen thought fast. There would be a lot of people at de Burgos's house — bodyguards and security. Carmen would have to tackle them eventually. But she wasn't going to miss an opportunity to confront Paperstar alone.

Carmen flattened herself against the stairwell, hoping

to take Paperstar by surprise. She closed her eyes and took a deep breath. Paperstar would be carrying the silver castle when she came down those stairs, and Carmen was going to steal it back from her.

It seemed like forever, waiting in the shadowy stairwell, hearing almost nothing above her — she could make out the occasional footstep overhead, but this far away she couldn't catch even a hint of conversation.

First came the hollow ringing of platform shoes on the metal steps. Then Carmen heard the singsong tune of Paperstar's humming, and finally the steps grew louder, and closer. Carmen moved to the middle of the stairwell just as Paperstar threw open the door.

"Going somewhere, Paperstar?"

Carmen savored Paperstar's shock. She was frozen in place, with her mouth in the shape of a very round *O*.

"Thought I was broken into sixteen pieces by now, huh?"

Paperstar straightened up. "I would be careful if I were you, Black Sheep — wouldn't want to injure yourself again after that kind of fall. Only an *amateur* takes a slip like that."

Carmen put her hand on her hip. "I tricked you, Paperstar. You know I did. So why don't you hand over the silver castle I know you're carrying now, before I embarrass you again."

Paperstar's eyes narrowed. "How sweet. Black Sheep thinks she can steal the silver castle from me. How would you do that when you couldn't even find a *dollar bill* to pass a final exam."

Carmen swallowed. The absolute worst moment of her time on Vile Island had been when she failed her final in stealth and discipline. Each VILE student had to find a dollar bill hidden somewhere in the professor's clothing. Carmen had watched the older students pass the final, one by one. She remembered how she had judged each of them, how they all missed obvious opportunities that she saw a mile away. Carmen had grown up on Vile Island, and she had been trained from birth to spot the kind of things VILE operatives needed to look out for. She had noticed when the other students missed a chance to lunge, or to duck and attack from behind. She had thought she was quicker and stealthier.

But when Carmen's turn had come, no matter how hard she tried, she hadn't been able to find the dollar bill. She did everything right—but she kept missing the dollar bill. The knowledge of her failure had haunted Carmen. There had been nights when she had woken up in a cold sweat after a nightmare about the exam day.

Paperstar edged past Carmen in the stairwell, and Carmen let her pass. "I didn't think you wanted to repeat that *particular* disaster," she said. "Good choice, Black Sheep. Ta-ta!"

Clearly, Paperstar was hoping that Carmen would be disarmed by the memory of her failures—and for a second, it worked. Carmen watched Paperstar retreating down the stairs. She took a deep breath.

And she remembered that there was more to the story. There were parts of the story that Paperstar didn't know, and would never know.

Carmen had realized that there never was a dollar bill—she hadn't found one because it was never hidden. The professor had failed Carmen on purpose. For a long time, knowing that didn't help Carmen get over the shame of failure. But she had spent the past year on caper after caper, using information she had gathered from VILE's stolen hard drive to stop their plans to steal treasures from around the world and make themselves richer. She had triumphed over VILE again and again.

Carmen squared her shoulders. She *had* been the best in her year. She knew that not because of some silly test, but because of what she had done after leaving VILE. Because of the evil she had managed to stop. Carmen had practiced all her life, and she had the stealth to find anything—and take it from anyone. With a furious roar, Carmen charged down the stairs after Paperstar.

Paperstar rounded the corner of the last bend in the stairwell, and Carmen leaped forward and latched onto her back just as Paperstar reached the ground-floor naval museum. Paperstar swung right and left, trying to shake Carmen, but Carmen clung tightly to her.

While Paperstar shook and jumped, trying to get Carmen off of her, Carmen methodically searched the pockets of Paperstar's jacket, hoping to find the silver castle. The silver was much too thick to be hidden in Paperstar's tight shorts, but Carmen wanted to be sure. She patted down Paperstar's thighs. Nothing.

"Get OFF of me!" Paperstar shouted, swinging so sharply that Carmen's grip loosened and she flew across the room, landing on her back near a display of brass barometers.

Carmen jumped to her feet and raced toward Paperstar. As Paperstar ducked to the right, Carmen tucked and rolled, grabbing Paperstar's platform boot as she slid across the floor. Paperstar tumbled to the ground with Carmen, and before she could retaliate, Carmen had pulled her left boot off her foot.

Frantically, Carmen turned the boot upside down, hoping the silver castle would shake free from the toe. Nothing.

Undeterred, Carmen tapped the rubber platform sole. It was certainly thick enough to hide a silver inlay. She peeled back the bottom layer of rubber, and Paperstar shrieked as if Carmen had ripped off a limb—but there was nothing in the platform of the boot.

Paperstar was now limping across the ground floor, trying to compensate for the difference in height between her bootless foot and her leg that was still raised by a three-inch platform. It only took Carmen two strides to catch up with her and yank off her jacket—she would deal with the other boot later—in the meantime, Paperstar couldn't get too far.

While Carmen searched the lining of the jacket, hoping to find a secret pocket or a patch sewn to the inside, bulging with silver, Paperstar leaped back to pick up her boot and jam it back on her foot. Carmen rolled her eyes. Let her have her boot, if it was that important to her. Carmen was determined to find the silver castle. She kept searching the jacket, but all she found were piles of folded paper.

The return of her left boot seemed to have a positive effect on Paperstar. Where she had been wretched and angry a minute ago, her smug calm was back. "Keep looking, Black Sheep. But I told you already—you're no good at this. You couldn't graduate from VILE Academy because you are just no good at stealth and discipline."

Carmen crouched on the ground, mentally searching every spot Paperstar could have hidden something.

Paperstar always dressed in sleek, posh outfits—there wasn't a lot of room for concealment.

"You thought just because you were the faculty's little baby Black Sheep—"

Carmen stood up suddenly. Something Paperstar had said—little baby Black Sheep—had just triggered a memory of a game Coach Brunt had played with her once when she was very young. They had been taking turns hiding a small doll—smaller than Carmen's palm—and finding it again. Then Coach Brunt had tried to hide it in Carmen's *hair.* Carmen remembered shrieking and giggling, because of course she could feel Coach Brunt's thick fingers pushing it under her ponytail. But it had also occurred to her then that tied-back hair could make a very good hiding place, indeed. Especially for something relatively flat and palm-shaped.

Carmen sized up Paperstar, whose signature two buns stuck out from her head like horns. They looked a little worse for wear after all the jumping and shaking and spinning they had done. Carmen looked for lumps or bulges, but Paperstar's hair was thick. The silver castle could well be hidden there, too deeply to see. Carmen would have to be deft.

"I actually *was* the faculty's little baby Black Sheep for a while," Carmen said. "You're right about that. But then I learned what they were really like, and I was done with that life." She moved gracefully toward Paperstar. "But you chose to stick around." Carmen leaned over Paperstar, resting her left arm on the doorframe.

Paperstar jerked her head away, and Carmen noticed for the first time that Paperstar had been holding her head a little to the left the entire night. It had blended in well with Paperstar's overall cocky, constantly questioning attitude, but it occurred to Carmen that maybe there was something heavy under Carmen's left bun. Something silver.

Carmen knew she would only have one guess. Pretending she was about to flick something off of her own shoulder, she raised her arm—and in one stroke she jammed her hand under Paperstar's left bun.

Paperstar yowled as Carmen's fingers closed around the silver castle. With her other hand Carmen loosened Paperstar's elastic, sending the hair on her left side of her head cascading over her shoulders— *Wow, her hair is long when it's not up in a bun,* Carmen thought—and freeing the silver shape. Carmen punched it into the air triumphantly, and while Paperstar whipped around, unable to see through the tangle of her own hair swinging in front of her, Carmen escaped the Torre del Oro and raced to meet her friends.

CHAPTER 18

C ARMEN EXPECTED THE PLAZA near Salvador de Burgos's house to be deserted. Even the latest of night owls had gone home, and she was hoping for a few moments to make a plan with Zack and Ivy before Paperstar showed up, probably with Le Chèvre and El Topo. Paperstar wouldn't have waited long before pursuing Carmen.

But instead of a quiet, deserted plaza, Carmen found a horse and an old-fashioned carriage decorated with flowers and lamps. The horse neighed hello when Carmen appeared.

"Evening, Carm," said Zack. "What do you think of our getaway vehicle?"

"It's, um, creative."

"That's what I said!" Ivy jumped down from the carriage and patted the horse's neck while Zack held the lead.

Ivy was dressed all in black, ideal for skulking and blending in, while Zack was dressed like a carriage driver in a white button-down shirt. "What's the plan, Carm?" Ivy asked.

Carmen held open her trench coat so Zack and Ivy could see the silver castle, securely fastened in place.

"Wow, Carm!" Ivy said. "Good work!"

"I managed to slow Paperstar down a little, but she won't be far behind, and Le Chèvre and El Topo are with her."

The horse neighed and Carmen bit her lip. "Don't you think the carriage draws attention?"

"Not at all," Zack said. "Just watch." He tipped his hat to an imaginary passerby. "A ride, milady? This carriage just dropped off the one and only Salvador de Burgos — he knows how to travel in style."

Carmen and Ivy burst out laughing.

"Okay," Carmen said, "I see your point." She turned to Ivy. "Ready?"

"Ready."

Carmen and Ivy crept toward the door. By Carmen's estimate, they had only a few minutes' lead on the VILE operatives, but if they could get inside and secure the door behind them, they would have time to locate the throne.

The door was not easy. It had one of the most sophisticated security systems Carmen had ever seen, with multiple sensors and locks.

"Definitely a job for Red Drone," Ivy said.

Carmen pulled the small red orb from her jacket, and together she and Ivy directed the drone to interact with the mansion's security system.

There was a lot more flashing and whirring than usual—Red Drone darted through the air from one part of the door to another, as if it were distracted or unfocused.

Ivy frowned. "Maybe Salvador de Burgos's house is Red Drone–proof?"

"Doubtful." But Carmen crossed her fingers just in case. She looked over her shoulder. *Let's get moving,* she thought.

"Red Drone disarmed the security system!" Player announced triumphantly, as the drone flew back toward Carmen, who caught it in her hand and tucked it back inside her jacket.

"We're in!" Ivy exclaimed. "I can't wait to look around without that guide boring us to death."

Carmen turned the knob, and the door opened easily. She and Ivy paused just inside the marble entry, but everything was silent and still. Red Drone had worked quietly, and no one knew they were there. Carmen shut the door behind them and turned the thumb lock. Ivy slid a deadbolt into place.

"We need something else to slow them down," Carmen whispered. "Now that we've turned off the security system."

Ivy tapped her temple as if to say, *One step ahead of you*. She lifted a heavy marble statue and set it down in front of the door. "That oughtta stop them."

Carmen leaned forward and checked the museum-style label on the pillar of the statue. "Made by a master sculptor in the seventeenth century. Fitting."

The doorknob turned, and outside Carmen and Ivy heard someone curse loudly. Le Chèvre.

"At least the lock is stumping them," Ivy whispered. "But let's get going!"

They ran through the elegant foyer, up the marble staircases, and through the grand rooms and hallways. When they reached de Burgos's study, they stopped to catch their breath. There was still no sign of VILE, and Carmen wondered whether they had figured out how to break through the deadbolt yet.

The study appeared empty. The velvet carpet sucked in all the sounds, giving the study an eerie, all-too-silent feel. The portrait of Salvador de Burgos looked stern and foreboding. His painting gave her an icy feeling all over—here was a man willing to cheat and lie for a few pounds of silver and a piece of furniture he liked.

"It's just past that bookcase." Carmen nodded toward the trick door.

"You think there's someone inside there?" Ivy asked.

"Hopefully Salvador de Burgos is sound asleep—"

"And hopefully his bodyguards stay in his bedroom," Ivy finished.

Carmen ran her fingernail along the groove in the bookcase and *ping!* open it swung.

The only problem was that de Burgos wasn't asleep, and his bodyguards weren't in his bedroom. All three of them were wide awake, standing in the private vault, and glaring angrily at Carmen and Ivy.

But that wasn't the bad part. The real problem was jumping down from the window ledge and into the vault: Le Chèvre.

"Did you forget my name, Black Sheep?" he asked delightedly. "I am The Goat, and I can climb anything I choose!"

Ivy and Carmen groaned. By disarming the alarm system, they had given VILE a chance to sneak into the mansion without either of them noticing.

One of the bodyguards reached back and gave Le Chèvre a hand. He then leaned out the window and hurled up a rope carrying El Topo, with Paperstar close behind. The three of them scrambled over the window ledge and faced Carmen and Ivy.

De Burgos cleared his throat. "Señorita Paperstar, the silver castle, please."

One of the bodyguards was ripping the tape off the refrigerator box with a box cutter, and Carmen watched his movements as she calculated their options.

"I don't have it," Paperstar said snarkily.

De Burgos did a double-take. "You don't—*pero,* I gave you *unprecedented* access to the Archivo! You would have never broken through their security without the insider knowledge I gave you, to say nothing of the equipment!"

"*She* has your silver castle." Paperstar pointed one of her deft fingers at Carmen.

Everyone swiveled in Carmen's direction.

Carmen's eyes narrowed. "The silver castle wasn't yours to take, Señor de Burgos. Neither was the throne."

"But—" Salvador de Burgos squinted at Carmen, as if he wasn't quite seeing her right. "You're my new servant! The señorita my dog Petra likes so much!"

The bodyguard finished ripping the tape off one side of the box, and through the gap in the cardboard, Carmen saw the sheen of the mahogany throne.

Carmen tipped her fedora. "Well, de Burgos, give back that throne and I'll be at your service."

"Héctor! Gonzalo!" de Burgos yelled sharply.

The bodyguards set down their box cutters and inched nervously away from Salvador de Burgos.

"How is it that a *thief* broke into my house? What do you think I'm paying you for!"

Being called a thief by someone who had just arranged for an international criminal heist was too much for Carmen. She fished the silver shape out of her jacket and held it high overhead. "Were you looking for this?"

Ivy gave her a puzzled look, but Carmen didn't actually have a plan. She was fueled by adrenaline and anger at Salvador de Burgos, at VILE for ruining everything for Milly—and all she knew was that she was sick of talking and ready to confront everyone in the room.

Woof-woof! Petra trotted into the room, carrying a bone in her mouth.

"Here, doggie," Ivy said, crouching down and holding out her hand.

Salvador de Burgos's eyes grew wide. "You . . . you bewitched my dog . . . and I won't let you lay a hand on her! Héctor! Gonzalo!"

Carmen thought fast. She grabbed Petra by the collar, reached into her jacket for a bandage, placed the silver castle on Petra's back, and wrapped it up snugly. "*Fuera*, Petra," she called. "Outside!" She loosened the bone from Petra's mouth and threw it down the hallway as hard as she could. Petra yapped wildly and took off running toward the bone.

Carmen straightened up and faced the VILE operatives and de Burgos's crew, all of whom were closing in on her and Ivy. "I would never hurt a dog," she snarled. "It's your thug friends you have to worry about."

There was a pause of only a few seconds, then, as if what they had seen was just dawning on them at that moment, Salvador de Burgos, his two bodyguards, Paperstar, Le Chèvre, and El Topo raced out of the private vault, through the study, and down the hallway.

"Here, girl!" shouted El Topo.

"I've got a treat for you!" Le Chèvre wheedled.

"Um, Carm?" asked Ivy when they were alone. "Aren't we worried they really do catch up with Petra? She's a pretty small dog?"

A wide smile spread across Carmen's face. She opened her jacket to reveal the silver castle, resting snuggly in its place.

CHAPTER 19

I VY'S MOUTH HUNG OPEN. "If you still have the silver castle, then what was . . ."

Carmen shrugged. "Silver paperweight off the desk out there." She jerked her finger in the direction of the outer study. "Come on, this won't be easy to move."

After a lot of grunting, they tipped the refrigerator box, with the throne inside, onto its side.

"Good thing de Burgos carpeted so well," Carmen said. "That'll pad things a little."

They rolled the box across the carpeted outer study. From down the hallway, they could hear everyone yelling to the dog, offering her treats, and cursing at her in turn. Now Carmen *really* owed Petra an extra-large bone.

At the top of the staircase, Carmen and Ivy locked eyes.

"We're going to have to lift it," Ivy said point-blank.

Together they tore off the cardboard box, scattering

packing peanuts onto the stairs. The throne was wrapped tightly in Bubble Wrap, but it would be easier to lift if Ivy grabbed the legs, so they tugged the Bubble Wrap down to expose the base and legs. The silver arrow shone, and on either side of it were the empty wooden spaces where the lion and castle belonged.

Ivy took the legs, and Carmen lifted the other end. They grunted as they carried the throne slowly down the stairs, and the sounds of the dog chase grew farther away.

Then suddenly there was an angry yowl, so loud that Carmen and Ivy stopped in place, four steps from the bottom. Carmen cocked her head to the side.

"CARMEN SANDIEGO!" It was Le Chèvre, screaming upstairs.

"Guess they found the decoy!" Carmen said cheerfully. "Let's move."

They brought the throne safely to the bottom of the stairs and stood it up just as Le Chèvre appeared at the top of the staircase. He shook his fist, and the others crowded around behind him. Salvador de Burgos was red in the face, and it looked like his neck might burst out of its collar. El Topo leered at them, and Paperstar reached into her pocket and sent darts slicing through the air. De Burgos's bodyguards tried to push through the crowd from behind, but Paperstar's unpredictable windups stopped them.

Le Chèvre started down the stairs, and Carmen had

to act fast. "Ivy, help!" There was a heavy wooden table in the foyer. Its plaque said something about finest oak, but Carmen didn't have time for reading right now. She and Ivy shoved as hard as they could and slid the table in front of the last step just as Le Chèvre hurtled to the bottom. He slammed into the desk and fell backwards, landing on his back. His head hit the marble and he yowled in pain.

"Help me!" Le Chèvre called. "Carmen Sandiego has killed me!"

"Oh, knock it off," Paperstar growled, forcing Carmen and Ivy to duck as her darts came fast and furious.

"Not much of a team player, is she?" Carmen said.

"Not much at all," Ivy remarked.

El Topo raced down the stairs to help Le Chèvre, while Paperstar kept up a volley of paper, forcing Ivy and Carmen to jump around as if the marble were hot lava. One of the paper darts hit a glass-blown vase and knocked it off of its pedestal. It broke into a thousand pieces.

"NOOOO!" Salvador de Burgos cried. He turned to his guards. "Héctor! Gonzalo! Save my precious things!"

The bodyguards closed in around Paperstar, pinning her arms to her sides.

"I'm on your team!" Paperstar screamed, kicking the bodyguards, but they held firm, marching her and her vase-breaking paper away from the stairwell while she shrieked and yowled.

Ivy leaped up onto the pillar of the statue they had shoved in front of the door and stood on tiptoe. She reached for two swords that were crossed over the doorway. She grasped one in each hand, jumped down from the pillar, and tossed one to Carmen.

"Anyone want to play now?" Carmen swung the sword right and left, enjoying the *whoosh*ing sound it made with each motion.

"Not my SWORDS!" Salvador de Burgos yelled. This time he himself scurried down the stairs, flapping his arms like a mother whose baby was in danger. "Those are encrusted with rubies! They are priceless works of art and—young ladies, I demand you replace them!"

"Not if you don't replace what you stole," Carmen replied. She pushed the statue out of the way, swung her sword overhead, and kicked the front door as hard as she could. The hinges shook, but the door didn't budge.

"I'll worry about the door, Carm, you worry about him!" Ivy pointed and Carmen whirled around.

De Burgos had hurled himself over his fine wooden desk and landed right in front of Carmen. He reached for the sword, but Carmen brought it straight down, and de Burgos jumped out of the way just in time—seconds later and the blade would have ripped his hand in two. He shrank away, but his eyes still flashed with anger.

Carmen held the sword an inch from de Burgos's face. She fixed him with an intense glare. "You think it's just *okay?*" she hissed. "You think you can just steal a throne because you want to feel important sitting on it?"

De Burgos held his hands up. "Señorita," he whimpered, "you don't understand. The people who had that throne didn't *appreciate* it."

"Oh, they appreciated it all right," Carmen said. "Do you know the curator at the museum was preparing to bring the throne to Bolivia for a special exhibit? Yeah. It was going to be the first time Bolivians would see the silverwork their ancestors created, and it was going to be the curator's first chance to see her father's country. You ruined that for her. How *dare* you."

De Burgos puffed out his chest, as if Carmen's words had empowered him instead of shamed him. "*Pero* a throne of this importance, that was sat on by a *king*—if they only understood!"

Carmen's eyes flashed. "A king who forced people to do horrible things just so he could make more and more money. Like someone else I know."

"*¿Quién?* . . . me?" De Burgos's eyes were wide and innocent. "I don't make money off of art, I spend money!" He put his hand over his heart. "As I told you yesterday,

I would *never* sell the Throne of Felipe. I stand by that promise."

"So you can pad your house with treasures that no one else gets to enjoy!" Carmen retorted.

"Why, I gave a public tour just yesterday!"

Carmen was scornful. "The first one in your entire life. I bet that was a cover-up, so the police wouldn't suspect you. Well, too bad, I'm about to let everyone know what you're up to. Carmen waved the sword around the first floor. "You just wanted to feel rich and important and you didn't care who you hurt in the process. Pathetic." Carmen thrust the sword forward, feigning an attack, and de Burgos jumped back. She walked steadily toward him, sword extended menacingly. "You stay right there."

"*Pero*—but—my *things!*"

Carmen turned her back on de Burgos.

"Yippee!" Ivy yelled. She had used an iron poker to slide open the door, and now their exit was wide open.

"NOOO!" Salvador de Burgos yelled again, but Ivy and Carmen lifted the throne, balanced the swords on top, and heaved it toward the door.

Outside, they set the throne down and slammed the door shut. "Phew, that thing is heavy," Ivy complained. "Zack!" she called, waving down the carriage. "Come help!"

Meanwhile Carmen was shoving the swords across the

doorway, creating a temporary jam. It wouldn't stop the likes of Paperstar, but Salvador de Burgos was too petrified of ruining the sword to try anything rash.

Zack met them, tipping his hat like a real carriage driver. "Got some luggage, I see. Hey, wait a second." He bent down. "You dropped something!"

Ivy clapped her hand over her mouth and Carmen knelt down. The silver arrow was lying on the ground a few inches from the throne.

"It fell off. I guess we set the throne down too hard."

"It *was* heavy," Ivy said.

Carmen scooped up the silver arrow tenderly, as if the shape were a living baby bird far from its mother. "It's okay," she said softly. "It's not even scratched."

Across the plaza, a pale glow spread out from the horizon. Sunrise had begun, and the day would soon be bright and warm. A ray of light fell on the spot where the silver arrow had lay just a moment ago, and Carmen glanced down.

There was a folded piece of paper. It fluttered slightly when a breeze came by. Without taking her eyes off the paper, Carmen tucked the silver arrow neatly inside her jacket, next to the silver castle. *Two out of three,* she thought. If only it could be three, for Milly's sake.

Carmen reached out and grabbed the folded paper.

"Carm!" Ivy said sharply. "Look!"

The metal blades of the two swords were bending like rubber. The doorknob shook.

"I guess de Burgos didn't like those swords as much as I thought," Carmen said.

"They're coming!" Zack shouted. "Run!"

Carmen scooped up the paper and raced after Zack, Ivy, and the heavy wooden throne. They heaved the throne inside the carriage, and Carmen and Ivy hopped in next to it as Zack shouted, "*¡Arre! ¡Arre!*" and the horse sprang into a canter.

The sound of the hooves was deafening, and the carriage, not built for these speeds, swung uncontrollably in different directions. It was all Carmen and Ivy could do to hold the throne securely in place.

But as they rounded the corner, Carmen sneaked one look behind her—the swords finally snapped, clattering to the ground—but VILE was far too late to catch them now.

"Player," Carmen called into her earpiece. "We'll be needing flights to New York, stat—with any luck we'll be there in time for Milly to prepare for the special exhibit in Bolivia—because *we got the throne!*"

"HOORAY!" Player shouted, so loudly that Carmen almost had to rip out her comm-link earring, and Zack and Ivy whooped and hollered in agreement.

CHAPTER 20

CARMEN HAD NEVER SEEN a carriage move so fast. Zack kept yelling, *"¡Arre! ¡Arre!"* which he confessed he had learned from the man who had lent him the carriage. "It's Spanish for 'giddyup,'" he explained." The horse maneuvered through the streets of Sevilla as if it were running from a fire. By the time they reached the city limits and turned onto an open country road, there was no sign of VILE. Zack jumped down from the driver's seat and patted the horse.

Now that they weren't going so quickly, the carriage ride became much smoother and more comfortable. Zack was leading the horse on foot to a farmhouse in the distance. Carmen was glad; this horse deserved some oats and water after their madcap escape from Sevilla.

"Carm," Ivy whispered.

Carmen lifted her head. It was hard to see Ivy over the throne's bulky shape.

"When are you going to look at that piece of paper?"

Carmen looked around. They were on a rough dirt road that Zack had found once they left the city. They were surrounded by leafy vineyards, gray-green and sprawling in every direction around them. The carriage kicked up dirt from the road, giving the morning a hazy, dusty feel. Carmen could see to the horizon, and they were completely alone. She reached into her coat and retrieved the paper.

It was folded tightly, with deep creases. The paper must have been pressed under the silver arrow for years, probably even centuries. Carmen unfolded it and spread it across her lap. It was a very official-looking kind of letter, with a great seal across the top.

Villa Imperial de Potosí it said in very large letters, with a coat of arms depicting two columns, and in between the columns, a shield decorated with castles and lions, flanked by wings on either side. A motto was written around the edge of the coat of arms — in Latin.

"How's your Latin, Ivy?" Carmen asked.

Ivy waved her arm majestically. "Oh yes, I learned it all in finishing school — I can tell you the root of the verb and the tense of the nouns." She giggled and dropped the act. "Can't help you there, Carm."

Carmen snapped a picture of the coat of arms. "Player?" she said into her earpiece.

"We found another clue as we were loading the throne, and we need some translation help. I don't know much Latin."

"Sometimes Latin is a lot like Spanish," Player said helpfully. "Did you try that?"

Carmen looked at the words on the coat of arms. There was "Rexis"—perhaps that was like *rey,* for king—but she didn't know much else. "I'm sending you the seal, can you get to work translating it?"

"Sure thing, Red."

Carmen examined the rest of the letter. She was pretty confident from the heading that it came from Potosí. But when she took a good look at the handwriting below the coat of arms, she gave a yelp of surprise.

"It's León de Mondragón! He wrote this!"

"Who's that?"

Carmen filled Ivy in on the silversmith León de Mondragón.

"I thought he shipped those inlays to Spain? When would he have been able to hide a letter in the throne?"

Carmen frowned. "I know León Mondragón visited Spain at some point." She filled Ivy in about the hidey-hole of León Mondragón's letters she had found beneath the AGI.

"So he was definitely here—"

"And when he was here, he hid all those papers beneath the AGI—"

"And put this letter behind the silver arrow!" Carmen's heart was fluttering and she felt a wild excitement. "It all makes sense. He would have had a good excuse for wanting to see the throne; he could just tell everyone he wanted to see what the silver shapes looked like once they were in place. Then once he was there, he found a moment alone—lifted off the shape—and slipped in this piece of paper."

"*Or,*" Ivy added, "they could have even asked him to fix something. He was the expert, after all. Then it would have been like they handed him an excuse to lift up that silver arrow."

"Yes!" Carmen said excitedly. It was all coming together now. León Mondragón had been the silversmith who had loved his work so much. He wanted to see it cared for properly. He hadn't liked that King Felipe IV had just wanted the silver shapes to sit at his feet and make him look good, hadn't properly appreciated the artistry, any more than Carmen liked Salvador de Burgos ferreting the throne away to feed his own ego. And he was trying to tell them something. Maybe the other clue had been a dead end—but maybe it had been a decoy. Maybe the silver lion hadn't vanished into thin air.

Maybe León Mondragón could still point Carmen in the right direction. She bent down and squinted at his dense handwriting.

The letter was in Spanish, but even though Carmen had a lot of practice with León's script at this point, there were tons of unfamiliar words. The letter was dated sometime late in the seventeenth century, and Carmen realized that it must have been toward the end of León Mondragón's life, and long after King Felipe IV had died. This was a letter meant for the people who would outlive Mondragón, a time capsule, a message in a bottle for the people of the future.

"What's it say, Carm?"

"I . . . there are a lot of words I don't know."

"I thought you knew a lot of Spanish? Didn't your nannies teach you all those languages?"

Carmen nodded. They had, but this was tricky. There were words sprinkled throughout that she had never seen before—she wasn't sure if they were even Spanish at all. Didn't León Mondragón speak another language?

They had reached the farmhouse, and Zack knocked on the door and asked for permission to let the horse use the family's stable. He parked them in a shady spot near the stable and led the horse to a water trough. Ivy wiped sweat from her forehead, and Carmen went back to examining the letter.

"Player?" she asked. "I'm having trouble reading everything this letter says."

"I'll run it through some of my translation software," Player said.

While she waited, Carmen concentrated on finding words she did know. She had been reading the same sentence over and over again, so she moved onto the next one. Eventually, a few words popped out to her.

"*Hurto,* that means stealing," Carmen said to Player. "And *españoles,* that means the Spanish."

"Sooo . . . he thinks the Spanish stole the silver?"

"Maybe?" Carmen said. She scanned the letter for more words she recognized.

Egoístas was repeated several times.

"He thinks they're greedy," Carmen told no one in particular. "He thinks the Spanish—or the king, I'm not sure who—he thinks they're selfish and greedy."

"Sounds about right," Player commented.

Carmen wrinkled her forehead. "But what are all these squiggles at the bottom of the letter?" León Mondragón—or someone—had drawn several lines. They looked somewhat like veins branching off from a central artery, and at the end of one of the lines was a little *x*.

X marks the spot, Carmen thought. Could there be treasure . . . or—she gulped—the remaining silver lion, hidden there? And if the squiggly lines were a map, what were they a map *of*—where was this place? She shook her head. She was getting ahead of herself. After all, León Mondragón had said that the silver lion had vanished into thin air. She shouldn't get her hopes up. Carmen steeled herself and decided that she would just tell Milly what she had found in Mondragón's hidey-hole below the AGI. She would tell her that the lion was gone—it had been lost, or destroyed, sometime far in the past, and neither VILE nor Carmen would ever find it.

Zack emerged from the stable and leaned casually against the carriage. "The farmer told me he can help get the horse back to its owner in Sevilla," he said. "Saves us an extra trip. Plus, he has a van we can borrow and leave at his daughter's apartment in Madrid."

"Nice guy," Ivy commented.

Zack tipped his hat. "We understood each other."

As if on cue, the farmer came out of the house carrying extra oats for their horse, and big bags loaded with snacks and water bottles for Carmen, Zack, and Ivy. They thanked him profusely and told him again and again that they would be okay, but he seemed determined to help the strangers who had come his way. He loaded them into his van, smiled happily, and slapped the dashboard as if saying, "*¡Arre!*"

Some people could be surprisingly generous, Carmen thought—and it made her even more angry to think that a farmer on the side of the road could want to give them his things and help them get to their destination safely while people like VILE members and Salvador de Burgos and the colonists in Potosí so many centuries ago just hurt people to make themselves richer and more important.

"Red," Player said into her earring, "I've got you on a flight back to New York City later today. Save that paper—I think Milly would want to see it."

CHAPTER 21

*P*LAYER!" Carmen hissed into her earring.

"What's the trouble, Red?"

The trouble was that they were halfway down a landing strip, headed to the private plane that would take them and the throne from Madrid to New York City, but someone was following them. She sensed movement behind her, like someone was tracking her footsteps, but every time she turned around they were gone. "Any intel, Player?"

"One second; I'm looking into air traffic controls and scanning aerial footage of the airports."

Hurry, Carmen thought. The hair on the back of her neck was prickling, and the odd feeling of being followed was just growing closer. It was hard to move quickly when she and Zack were wheeling the heavy throne on a hand truck. Ivy was trying the tactic of turning around and shouting "Gotcha!" every few moments, hoping to scare whoever it was away, but Carmen didn't think it was a winning strategy. Meanwhile, Zack was too loaded down with Spanish ham to be of much help. He said he wasn't going to eat anything else for months.

"Hmm," Player said, "an undisclosed organization reserved a take-off time on the landing strip next to ours. But it doesn't say where they're going."

Carmen groaned. Because they didn't *know* where they were going. It was VILE. They were planning on tailing them.

"You'll have to shake them once you get to New York, Red. I don't see any other way around it."

Player was probably right — there was no use putting up a fight in midair; none of them were prepared for that and it would probably get them killed. But Carmen wanted to meet Milly and get to the bottom of the letter from León Mondragón. Fighting VILE in New York would be a huge distraction.

Unless. Carmen stopped in her tracks. An idea took hold in her mind. She remembered once holding off VILE with decoy Carmens — to be specific, Zack and Ivy dressed in red trench coats and fedoras. Instead of following the real Carmen, VILE had gotten mixed up and followed Zack and Ivy in their red trench coats all around the city before realizing they had been led awry. VILE probably wouldn't fall for decoy Carmens again, but that didn't mean they couldn't be waylaid by another kind of decoy.

"Player," Carmen asked. "Could you reserve a landing spot for us that's the same general direction as New York—but definitely *not* New York?"

While Player worked on picking a location, Carmen spotted a maintenance building by the landing strip. She jerked her head in its direction, and she and Zack and Ivy maneuvered the throne inside the building's bathroom.

"Don't want to be overheard," she said, moving away from the door and closer to the toilet for safe measure.

"Um, Carm?" Zack said. He was holding his nose. "This really isn't the best place for a meeting. I'm worried the smell might hurt my ham."

Ivy rolled her eyes and Carmen went ahead and explained the plan. When they were all on the same page, they returned to the landing strip, walking slowly and chatting breezily. When Carmen was pretty sure someone was only steps behind her, certainly in earshot, Ivy said cheerfully, "The weather in Kalamazoo will be lovely this time of year."

"Oh yeah," Carmen agreed loudly. "Plus, who knew that the world's greatest silver depository was in Kalamazoo, Michigan? We're going to have a lot to *look through* when we get to Kalamazoo."

"We won't waste any time when we land," Ivy agreed. "We'll just be business, business, business in Kalamazoo."

They had chosen Kalamazoo, Michigan, because it was generally west of Madrid, just like New York City, but also because they loved the name. Now Carmen worried it was too obvious — they were having too much fun saying Kalamazoo at every turn.

"You know, Kalamazoo is quite a destination," Ivy said, a few feet from the plane. "Too bad we'll be in and out within the hour — we're not going to waste any time in Kalamazoo."

Feeling she would be lucky if Ivy didn't entirely give up the ghost, Carmen grabbed Ivy's wrist and urged her onto the jet plane while Zack secured the throne in back and climbed up to the cockpit. "Come on," Carmen said. "We can't waste any time getting to Kalamazoo."

Carmen, Zack, and Ivy strapped in for their flight. In minutes, they were airborne. "Come on, come on, come on," Carmen said to herself.

"YES!" Player shouted into her earring, and Carmen, Zack, and Ivy did little seat-dances from thirty thousand feet. A private plane had just streaked by them, headed west much farther and faster than they were — with someone who looked suspiciously like Le Chèvre in the pilot's seat.

CHAPTER 22

NEW YORK CITY WAS AS LIVELY AS EVER, and despite the brand-new refrigerator box they were carrying with them, Carmen, Zack, and Ivy blended into the crowd as they made their way from the airport to the subway station. Ivy had wanted to take a cab with the heavy throne, but Player's GPS showed that traffic was horrendous, and they couldn't risk having their movements tracked by a ride-hailing app. So they maneuvered the throne down the packed stairwell into the dimly lit station. It had once been an elegant station, but now tiles were missing from the pattern on the wall that announced the stop, and someone had taken a Sharpie and scrawled rude things over the posters advertising movies and shows. All the same, they enjoyed the clatter of many languages being spoken around them, all in tones that revealed people happy to be home or excited to be visiting the largest city in the United States.

"Did you know the New York City subway system has more stations than any metro or subway in the world?" Player asked. "You could spend ages trying to get to all of them."

Zack was bouncing on the balls of his feet, peering down the dark tunnel.

"Going to try and drive the subway too?" Ivy asked, with a smirk.

"As if," Zack said. "I'm going to be a T conductor—in *Boston,* of course, the country's *first* subway system!" But as the train drew into the station, he hustled forward. "Let's sit near the conductor—I gotta watch."

Friendly strangers made space for them as they heaved the box onto the train, and then it sped off into the pitch-black tunnel. Luckily, the subway car was full of unusual people doing unusual things—there was a woman playing a ukulele and singing off-key, a man putting his hair in curlers, and someone dressed up as a vampire princess, although it was nowhere near Halloween. No one seemed to mind that Carmen and Ivy were holding an enormous box. People probably moved refrigerators on trains all the time in New York City.

It was a long ride up to Washington Heights, not to mention they had to switch trains. By the time they reached their stop, they had watched dozens, maybe even hundreds, of people get on and off the train around them.

Ivy had gotten a seat and fallen asleep with her head on the side of the refrigerator box. She was snoring slightly. Carmen shook her awake. They had arrived.

Their hand truck was useless on the stairs, so they were all sweating by the time they reached the top of the subway entrance. They heaved the refrigerator box up the last step and set it down on the sidewalk. Zack leaned on it and fanned his face. It was a good thing the museum was only a few steps away, because Carmen wasn't sure how much longer they could handle the heavy box.

The terrace was all but deserted. It was nearly five o'clock in the afternoon, and visitors had gone home for the day. By the looks of the sleepy guard by the door, the museum wasn't expecting much more activity. When Carmen explained they were there to see Milly, he smiled indulgently and waved them inside.

Carmen, Zack, and Ivy carried the throne up the stairs and wove their way through the galleries to Milly's office. They knocked on the door.

Milly opened it. She looked terrible. She had a strained appearance and bags under her eyes, like she had been working overtime and maybe doing some crying. Her office was, if it was possible, messier than before. Now even her desk was piled with clutter, and the picture of her father was obscured by a long and official-looking report.

"Oh," said Milly when she saw them. "It's you three again."

Carmen faltered. She had been imagining Milly's expression the entire plane ride home. In her imagination, Milly had been grateful and overjoyed. Carmen had pictured her saying, "I knew you would get it back all along! I had complete faith in you. I wasn't even a little bit worried!" But clearly Milly *had* been worrying, and clearly she did not have complete faith in Carmen.

"We, um . . . brought you something."

Milly raised an eyebrow.

"Ta-da!" said Zack. He waved his arms in front of the refrigerator box like a game show anchor unveiling the prize car.

Milly's face was completely blank. Then she sighed. "Is that a replacement throne? That's the second one I've been offered this week."

Carmen looked at Zack and Ivy. "No," she said slowly, shaking her head. "You misunderstood—it's not a *replacement.*"

Milly was now nodding sympathetically at Carmen, the way Coach Brunt used to do when Carmen made her bracelets out of string as a kid, or failed breakfast-in-bed attempts. It made Carmen's face burn.

"It's very nice of you," Milly went on, forcing a smile.

"But of course, what mattered about the throne were the original inlays—"

Zack interrupted. "That's what we've been trying to tell you! We have the throne *and* the inlays!" And without waiting for Milly to reply, he reached into his jeans, flipped up the blade of a pocketknife, and ripped open the box. The cardboard fell away, leaving the throne, heavily encased in Bubble Wrap. It looked like a moth swaddled in its cocoon. But even through all the layers, it was plain what was inside. The silver arrow still twinkled within.

Milly put her hands over her mouth. For a moment, no one said anything. When Milly lowered her hands, there were tears in her eyes. She reached an arm out silently, and Zack, understanding her meaning, handed her the pocketknife. Milly started at the bottom, running the pocketknife up through the layers of Bubble Wrap as if she were unzipping a winter sweater. When the whole base was uncovered and the silver castle was revealed, newly polished and shining next to the silver arrow, she dropped to her knees and pushed her face very close. Carmen could practically see her heart glowing. This was better, much better than any praise Milly could have given them.

When the throne was safely inside Milly's office, Milly reached for the phone. She was frantic to contact her colleagues in Bolivia and tell them that the special exhibit would be happening after all, and to call her father's relatives and tell them that, at long last, she would get to meet them in person. But after the calls had been made and the happy crying and shouting had subsided, Carmen retrieved the folded letter from her pocket.

She laid it out on Milly's desk, on top of all the paper and clutter. Milly unfolded her reading glasses. While Carmen explained about finding León Mondragón's secret hiding spot in Sevilla, Milly examined the letter carefully.

"But the problem," Carmen said, finishing her long story, "is that I can't read this letter. I feel like it might have a clue, but I can't tell for sure. All I can make out is something about how the Spanish were selfish—and how they stole the silver."

Milly put down the letter and folded her arms. She looked steadily at Carmen. "What do you think, Carmen? Did the Spanish steal the silver?"

Carmen considered for a minute. "On the one hand, León Mondragón got paid for making those silver inlays; I saw the accounts he kept myself. Player—that's my friend—" Carmen added quickly, not wanting to explain any further, "told me that in seventeenth-century money, he was paid really well. But on the other hand, the ore was mined and the silver was refined by people who were forced to work and who weren't paid enough to even cover the supplies they needed to do the job—that *is* like stealing, when you think about it. Like stealing from the mountain itself."

Milly glanced at a framed print hanging on her wall, one Carmen hadn't noticed before. It was a rough engraving of the side of a mountain, and it looked almost as if the mountain had been split open to reveal the contents inside. It showed workers climbing up and down, following the veins of ore with heavy packs on their backs.

"The Red Mountain," she said wistfully. "They say that from a distance the minerals in the ground make it look reddish. Some people called it the Cerro Rico too—the Rich Hill. But for everyone it made wealthy, someone else was injured or killed in the mines, or spent months, or years, away from their family in constant danger. They would force them to work all night, even when they knew there was a risk of a cave-in." Milly shuddered at the thought. "I would say it's fair to call what happened in those mines stealing." She pushed her reading glasses farther up her nose. "But, Carmen, of course you didn't understand all of the words in this letter—they're not all in Spanish."

"They're not?"

"No, of course not. Think about it. Remember how I told you that the smith who made these silver inlays was mestizo—half Spanish, half Lupaca? That meant that he was probably bilingual, and likely even trilingual. He spoke Spanish like his father, of course, but he also spoke Quechua, which was the language of the Incas —the Indigenous empire that ruled the region before the Spanish—and likely another Indigenous language, Aymara. I think these words are from those languages."

"So can you read 'em?" Ivy asked eagerly.

"I'll take a stab at it," Milly said with a little laugh. "Some of my friends from Bolivia speak Aymara, but I've only ever picked up a little." She studied the letter a little longer, her mouth moving ever so slightly as she read. Finally, she leaned back and pulled off her reading glasses.

"It sounds like that trip to Spain in his old age changed a lot for León Mondragón," she explained. "Once he visited the court of King Felipe IV and saw where his silver crafts were installed, he no longer thought of shipping his work around the world like making a connection to life beyond the mountain. The greed he witnessed! The courtiers didn't care at all what kind of skill went into making the silver shapes. They weren't interested in how he combined silversmithing techniques from Europe and the Andes. All they cared about was how valuable the silver was. They were ready to melt it down! Imagine!"

Carmen could not, for the life of her, imagine melting

down anything as fine and detailed as the silver arrow—not unless someone's life depended on it—but she knew plenty of people in VILE who would be only too glad to do so.

"Mondragón came to believe that all that work he had done—all of the skill he had honed and all of the sweat and passion he had put into making silver shapes—was for nothing. People weren't taking joy from looking at his craftsmanship; they only saw money. They didn't appreciate the hard work that went into it. He decided that in his whole life, he had done nothing but make money for the colonists." Milly glanced down at the letter one more time and bit her lip. "He started to think the silver should have stayed in Potosí. He almost regretted having been a silversmith. But most of all, he was angry at Joaquín Reinoso."

"The merchant who built the tunnels?"

Milly nodded. "It seems like León Mondragón caught on to him—and that the silver castle was stolen during Mondragón's trip to Spain. Of course, people clamored for Mondragón to make a replacement, but he refused. He was done working for the Spanish. He only wanted to work for himself, for the rest of his life." Milly shook her head. "He doesn't say how, but he traced the theft of the silver castle to the merchant Joaquín Reinoso. In this letter—really it's more of a diary, it's not addressed to anyone—he's so furious. That someone would steal his work and hide it away was too much for Mondragón."

Carmen cleared her throat. "Milly?" she asked. "There's something I don't get. So León Mondragón was mad at Reinoso for squirreling away the silver castle—and then Mondragón decided to destroy the silver lion—so that *no one* would ever get to see it again? That just doesn't make sense."

CHAPTER 23

THE ROOM WAS QUIET while everyone considered what Carmen had said.

"What makes you think Mondragón destroyed his silver lion?" Milly asked.

Carmen told her about the other note she had found, hidden below the Archivo in Sevilla. Mondragón had told everyone not to bother looking for it, because it had vanished. "But now that you're reading us this other letter—it sounds like *he* was the one who made it vanish. Because he didn't want it to be in Spain, where people saw his art as just money."

Milly nodded. "It's interesting, isn't it?"

Carmen knew exactly what Milly meant. "That he chose the lion to take—because his name was León. It's almost like he was talking about himself—like *he* belonged back on the mountain, and not in Spain."

Ivy brought everyone back down to reality. "So he vanished himself? That doesn't make much sense."

"But for the Spanish—for the people who would have found that note if it had been discovered behind the arrow centuries ago instead of just now—he *had* vanished, right?" Then Carmen shook her head. "I guess it doesn't get us any closer to finding the silver lion."

Milly smiled placidly. "Carmen, the throne returned—and the two silver shapes—seeing the silver castle in person, it's already more than I ever expected. I thought when the throne was stolen it was gone for good. You've done very, very well, and you should be proud of yourself. Of course, I don't know *how* you did it . . ."

Carmen gave Milly a mysterious look. "Don't ask a lady to reveal her secrets."

Milly laughed. "All right, I won't, then. But don't let that silver lion bother you too much. *No pasa nada.* You've done well."

Carmen continued pacing around the tiny amount of space in Milly's office. There was something that didn't quite fit. It was like having an itch somewhere you couldn't reach; the answer was there, somewhere, but she couldn't put her finger on it. She just knew there was something flitting around the edges of her mind, nagging her not to be forgotten.

She turned sharply toward Milly. "Could I show you the other clue?" she said abruptly.

"Of course," Milly said. "Although it sounds like you and your friend Player have done all the sleuthing you need."

"We don't have the original clue anymore," Carmen explained, "but I can show you the photo we took of it."

"What happened to the original?"

Carmen shifted her weight. She wasn't about to tell Milly about VILE. "Lost," she said. She pulled out her phone and sent Milly the photo, which Milly loaded onto her computer. They all gathered around to have a good look. Zack and Ivy hadn't seen it yet.

Milly leaned forward. "Carmen!" she said, very suddenly. "He doesn't say the silver lion vanished! Not at all!"

Carmen frowned. Had her translation been completely wrong? Milly obviously had a lot more practice reading old documents; she was reading the note in the footer as if it had been neatly typed.

"He said it vanished *into thin air.*" Milly held her hands out as if to say, *Don't you see?*

But Carmen didn't see. "So it's gone, right?"

"No." Milly shook her head, grinning wildly. "Think about it, you three. León didn't like being in Spain. He was mad about the treatment his artwork received there.

So he took the lion and said that it had vanished—*into thin air.* Where in the world is there thin air?"

Slowly, it dawned on Carmen. "Thin air—when you're high up in the mountains, the air is thin!" she said excitedly. "That's why people get altitude sickness!"

Milly jumped up and gave Carmen an impulsive hug. "We know where the silver lion is! It's in Potosí!"

Zack coughed. Carmen and Milly whirled around to face him.

"Not to be a party pooper," he said, "but didn't you all say Potosí was a big city? How are we going to find it?"

But Carmen was one step ahead of him. "He left a map. Look!" She pointed to the spidery lines at the bottom of the letter, and the tiny *x* at the end of one of the veins.

"*¡Dios mío!*" Milly said in a hushed voice. "I can't believe it—this is a map, Carmen! And look at that seal— this is a map of the Cerro Rico mines, I'm sure of it . . . I bet this will lead us right to the silver lion!"

CHAPTER 24

ARMEN, MILLY, ZACK, AND IVY climbed down from their plane and stepped onto the tarmac at El Alto International Airport.

Carmen's first thought was that Bolivia was *loud*—though they were on an isolated tarmac, she could hear traffic rushing by and smell exhaust fumes from cars and trucks. But when she glanced at Milly, the honking and clattering seemed suddenly far away. Milly breathed in deep. She was here, Carmen realized. The place her people had come from, and the place she had never been to before. Carmen wondered if this is what she would feel like when she visited Buenos Aires—whether her face, too, would reflect Milly's serene appearance.

But the moment was fleeting, and before long a different kind of noise greeted them: what looked like about a dozen people, rushing toward them and happily waving their arms.

"Milagros!" cried a very old, short woman. *"¡Aquí estamos!"* She reached Milly ahead of the others and threw her arms around her neck. Milly started sobbing.

"Titi Ana," she repeated over and over again, and buried her face in the woman's neck. After what seemed like a long time to Carmen, who stood guarding the throne and keeping an eye out for signs of VILE, Milly pulled back, wiped her eyes, and gazed at the woman.

"No lo creo," Milly said. "I don't believe it." She turned to Carmen, Zack, and Ivy, still holding the older woman around the shoulders. "This is my Titi Ana," she explained. "My father's favorite aunt. When I was a kid, she would call us up in New York every time she had the money for long distance—" And that was as far as Milly got before the two of them dissolved once more into tears and hugs.

It must be something, Carmen thought, *to have relatives.* People who would meet you at the airport with smiles and tears even if you hadn't ever seen each other in person. People who loved you even if you were thousands of miles away. Thinking about family made Carmen's eyes sting; it wasn't fair that the only family she had ever known was an international band of criminals, people who wouldn't hesitate to push her off a cliff if it would help them steal a treasure and make a buck. Someday, maybe Carmen would find a real family, people like those that now crowded around Milly. Until then, she would keep fighting VILE. She would protect people like Milly from their horrible antics.

Milly was now dabbing her eyes with the end of her sleeve and introducing the rest of her relatives, even as she met them herself. While they hugged and kissed her and patted her on the back, she told Carmen, Zack, and Ivy their names and a little bit about who they each were. "This is my cousin Luis, he works as a tour guide here in town; and this is Lila, my father's sister; and this is my uncle Carlos, Ana's son, but my dad always used to call him Chachi."

Chachi was tall and strong, the exact opposite of Milly's tiny Titi Ana. He tipped his baseball cap to them, and Milly rapidly explained that Chachi was going to be helping them get to Potosí. He ran his own construction business and made frequent runs to Potosí, so it was no problem to pile Carmen and her friends into his truck. On the way to the mines, they would drop Milly off at the Casa de la Moneda, the old mint where coins had once been made in Potosí. It was now a museum, and it was there that Milly would be meeting her museum colleagues to set up the exhibit with the throne. They would set up the special exhibit there—but not until Carmen had her chance with León Mondragón's map.

All too soon, it seemed to everyone, Carmen, Zack, and Ivy were crammed in the back of Chachi's truck. Milly hopped into the passenger seat next to Chachi, and they waved goodbye to her family, who would meet them later in Potosí.

While Milly was busy catching up with Chachi and sending text messages to the museum people, updating them on the location of the throne, Carmen had time to enjoy the landscape around them. Even though the drive went on for hours, she wasn't bored. They crossed a long plateau, passed a salt lake that looked almost as if it were made of glass, and climbed over a desolate mountain range. Carmen pulled her sweater around her more tightly. As the truck clambered higher, they passed canyons below them and tall industrial trucks that Carmen was sure were loaded with ore.

"Chachi," Carmen said, as they turned sharply on a mountain switchback and readied for another steep curve, "I feel fine this time—I haven't gotten altitude sickness."

Chachi spoke to them in Spanish, with Carmen translating for Zack and Ivy. "Altitude sickness can be like that," he said. "Sometimes you get it, and sometimes you don't. It can go either way, even for the same person."

Grateful to be feeling well, Carmen tried to enjoy the sweeping views from the window of the truck. Chachi rolled down the window and the rumbling sound was louder than ever, but Carmen craned her neck out to see even further.

"You'll be reaching the city of Potosí any minute now," Player said to Carmen through her earring.

"Player," Carmen said quietly, hoping not to be over-heard by anyone else in the truck. "There's something that's bugging me—we haven't seen any sign of VILE since the airport—it's making me nervous."

"Hmm." Player was thoughtfully silent. "Maybe our decoy really worked? They flew to Kalamazoo?"

"Wouldn't they have figured it out by now? They would have had time to get here from Michigan already, and the return of the throne and the special exhibit have been in the papers. I can't imagine they would just give up like that."

"I'll do some digging," Player said. "In the meantime, keep an eye out for anything suspicious."

"I always do," Carmen replied, resignedly. She fell silent as the truck continued to rumble and clatter and drive up the mountain.

After a while, Ivy leaned forward beside her. "Look! We're almost there!"

They were fast approaching the city of Potosí. The first glance gave Carmen a chaotic impression, she saw a jumble of old and new: apartment buildings in colorfully painted concrete with shiny glass windows, and farther away terra-cotta tiles and the bell towers of an old stone cathedral.

"Check it out!" Zack pointed. "It really is red!"

Carmen looked and saw the famed Cerro Rico — the Red Hill, the hill of treasure — rising up behind the city. It was somehow flatter and more spread out than she had imagined it; of course they were already at a high altitude. The Cerro Rico was brownish, but with a distinctive red tint.

"Red," Player said conversationally, "did I tell you I found out what was on that coat of arms on León Mondragón's letter? It was Latin, and the motto of Potosí: *I am rich Potosí / treasury of the world / king of mountains / and envy of kings.*"

Carmen bit her lip and looked out through the front windshield. In the space between Milly and Chachi, she could see that they were going through an archway, straight into the old terra-cotta part of town. It all gave her a very strange feeling. On the one hand, she felt excited butterflies in her stomach, to be reaching this fabled place, whose treasures had changed the world in so many ways, and where people like León Mondragón had worked and followed their passions and loved their families. On the other hand, she felt nauseous thinking about all of the greed and selfishness that the mines had brought out in people throughout the ages, in the kings and colonists from Spain, in the merchant who ferreted treasures away in his secret vaults, in Countess Cleo and the other people at VILE, who would do anything for more riches. Carmen had almost become one of them. She had come so dangerously close to living a life of crime. She took a deep breath and looked around at Zack and Ivy, then tapped her earring. Carmen didn't know how she felt about Potosí—about whether it was a rich place, a city to be envied like the coat of arms boasted, or a poor and sad place, a city she should revile—but she did know she was grateful to have escaped a life of international evil and to have found these friends to do some good with.

They dropped Milly off at the Casa de la Moneda, where a group of museum curators greeted her and helped her lower the box with the throne out of the truck. The outside of the Casa de la Moneda reminded Carmen vaguely of the AGI in Sevilla, and one of the cathedral's bell towers rising behind it completed the picture.

Then Milly was kissing them all goodbye, and they were off again, headed full speed toward the Red Mountain.

CHAPTER 25

ARMEN SHARED MONDRAGÓN'S MAP with Chachi, and he turned it every which way before deciding that the mine opening Mondragón suggested was way up near the peak. He didn't seem entirely confident, but Carmen had to trust him. She didn't have any other leads.

"You should wait down here," Carmen told Zack and Ivy. Keep an eye out for anything suspicious, and if you see VILE—"

"Don't worry, Carm," Zack said, "We'll stop them."

Carmen nodded apprehensively. She would be on high alert until the silver lion was safely in her own possession. It just didn't seem like VILE to turn around and go home unless it was really and truly the end of the line for them.

Gratefully, Carmen accepted Chachi's loan of a hard-hat, a headlamp, and a pickaxe. "Everything you need but the dynamite," he said with a chuckle. Then his face grew serious. *"Cuidado,"* he said. "Climbing into an abandoned mine is extremely dangerous. I wouldn't let you, but Milagros says we need to trust you." Then he helped Carmen hide her hair under her hardhat. *"Y tú una señorita."* He shook his head. "Women aren't supposed to go into the mines. It's bad luck—*mala suerte.*"

"I don't think I really have a choice," Carmen said apologetically. "It's something to help Milly. And it's important."

Chachi nodded solemnly, patted Carmen on the back, and wished her luck. Carmen thought again how fortunate she was that Milly and her family were willing to help—even if they thought she was doing something reckless.

As she left her friends behind and made her way slowly up the mountain, Carmen must have made a strange sight. Chachi's hardhat hid her hair, but she needed the tools in her red trench coat, so she hardly looked like a regular miner. Luckily, the dusty dirt roads were mostly empty, and she passed only a few miners, too focused on their heavy packs to notice her. Every once in a while, she went by a single-story cement structure with a tin roof, where miners were changing gear or stocking up on juice and other supplies. About halfway to the top, she saw an old man walking next to a llama on a lead. Carmen nearly said *aww* out loud—the llama was fluffy and wooly, with a long neck and comically oval-shaped ears. She loved it instantly, and wished she had time to stop and chat with the man leading the llama along.

Near the top, she stopped to examine the map once more. It didn't really show *where* on the mountain to enter; instead it showed the gallery itself and the different turns she would have to take to reach the right spot. So Carmen prowled the top of the mountain, looking at the dark holes that led down below, wondering which one to take.

In the end, it was fairly easy. The newer entrances were crisscrossed with wires and pipes, and some of them were even decorated with colorful paper and ribbons. Carmen was looking for an entrance that hadn't been used for hundreds of years, and she found it, plain and unmarked, a great black hole on the side of the mountain.

It was like lowering oneself into the belly of a terrible monster, and for a wild second Carmen wanted to close her eyes, but she forced herself to switch on her headlamp and focus.

It was much, much worse than any tunnel she had ever explored. She had to duck almost immediately, and thick dust clogged her nose and eyes. She dug a handkerchief out of her coat and covered her nose and mouth, but she wasn't sure how much it helped. The headlamp only showed a little way ahead of her, and the height of the gallery varied widely from step to step — one minute she could walk along, stooped over, another minute she would be nearly squatting to avoid bumping her head on the rough rock above her. Where the gallery met another long tunnel, like two roads intersecting, Carmen noticed tracks running along the ground, likely to transport carts of ore in and out of the mine. There was also a statuette of a demon-like figure, covered in colorful strings and soda cans.

"Player?" Carmen asked curiously. "Any idea what I'm looking at?"

Player cleared his throat. "El Tío," he said, "is the demon of the mines. It says here that miners leave him colorful offerings to *'alejar el mal*—'"

"To keep away bad things," Carmen finished for him. "Like VILE, I hope." She fished in her jacket for something to leave him, but the best she found was a pack of multicolored sticky notes. Carefully, she arranged them around the strings and bottles.

She could stand up straight in this intersection, and she took a minute to look around. On the sides of the crossing gallery, she could see holes where miners had blasted dynamite to widen the mine. She took another peek at Mondragón's map and confirmed that she would follow the older shaft for quite a while. She plunged forward, and before long she came to a rickety ladder, leading down, deep into the lower levels of the mine. She had no choice but to lower herself. But luckily, Carmen could scramble with the best of them. She was nimble and balanced, and quickly reached the bottom of the ladder, where things evened out once more.

She pulled the map out of her pocket and examined it. She should be looking for a narrow turn, by the looks of it about fifty paces from where she now stood. Determined, she walked forward.

If she hadn't been looking so carefully, the turn would have been easy to miss. It was more of a sliver than a hole, and Carmen grazed the walls of the mine as she slipped inside the narrow channel. It was somehow even darker here; any sunlight from above had long been blocked by the twists of the mine, and in these narrow quarters, Carmen's headlamp didn't reflect very far. She took things step by step.

A few times, as she walked slowly down the pitch-black tunnel, Carmen thought she heard a sound above—something like humming, an almost angelic, vibrating song, coming from another part of the mine. Perhaps one of the miners, somewhere deep in another gallery, was singing to themselves. Perhaps some of the miners were women, whose beautiful voices kept everyone feeling safe. It was a comforting thought.

The map instructed Carmen to turn again, and she found herself facing a short ledge with an opening so tiny there was no way in but to army crawl. Carmen took a deep breath, climbed onto the ledge, and lowered herself onto her stomach. She wriggled along slowly, now wishing she had taken a better look at the map before entering this narrow opening—it would be very difficult to check the map in such a space. As it was, Carmen could barely move her arms. Her coat snagged on a rough patch of rock and tore at the elbow.

The humming sound was closer now, and Carmen took a steadying breath. She was sweating in the hot, stuffy air. But she was nearly there. And she was lucky— she was in this mine because she wanted to be, because she was searching for treasure. She had a map, a guide from long ago. So many others, now and then, came to this mine because they had no choice. *Lucky*, Carmen told herself, even as the raw skin of her elbow scratched the wall again, leaving a streak of blood on her jacket. *Almost there. Almost.* She heaved herself forward another few feet, and mercifully found herself facing a gentle slope down to the sudden widening of the tunnel.

Carmen wriggled down the slope on her stomach and straightened up. She dusted herself off and tugged at her coat sleeve, pulling the fabric over her cut. She was in a small cavern, not much taller than she was, but large compared to the other channels she had explored. It was maybe three feet across—really just big enough for one person. On one side was the entrance she had just taken, and on the other it was crossed by a wide gallery that led downhill, even deeper into the mountain. It was one of the galleries where tracks had been laid, and there were three or four empty carts in sight. She noted that the carts were held in place by a large rock; otherwise gravity would have sent them careening down into the shaft.

Carmen put her hands on her hips. She was fairly certain this was the spot where the X was marked on her map, but the map was so vague it was hard to tell. She paced from one end of the cavern to the other, which took about three steps each direction.

The trouble was, the cavern was just big enough that Carmen couldn't reasonably dig up the entire place. Or if she did, it would take the rest of the day and most of the night. The special exhibit was supposed to open the next day.

"Any ideas, Player?" Carmen asked.

"I think León Mondragón wanted someone to find this lion," he said. "Not just anyone, of course, but the right person—someone who really understood what it meant to him. Otherwise he would have never left a map, or any notes, when you think about it."

"Am I the right person?"

"Do you understand him?"

Carmen thought of all of the writing she had read

by León Mondragón, how his early notes had reminded her of herself, seeking a connection to a world outside his mountain like she had wanted a connection to a world outside her island. Talking to Player had been that for Carmen — it had given her not only a link to life beyond Vile Island but, ultimately, her freedom. Friendship with Player hadn't just given her a window, a thread to tie her to experiences beyond the island; it had thrown open the door and granted her the chance to actually be out there, and on her own terms, *not* Coach Brunt's or Professor Maelstrom's.

But for León Mondragón, things hadn't worked out quite so well. For a while, when he was young, his silver-smithing was his lifeline to the world beyond Potosí. He got to correspond with powerful people far away, and send a little bit of himself — his talent and artistry, the skills he had learned from each side of his family — to places far off and important. It had been, for a while, an honor. Until one day, it stopped looking like an honor to Mondragón. It started looking to him like the kings and merchants for whom he had once crafted commissions were greedy and cunning. Maybe he had always known that somewhere inside, like Carmen had always known somewhere inside that VILE was not a real family. But once he visited Spain and experienced the king's court, once he realized what the merchant Joaquín Reinoso was willing to do to add to his riches, it became impossible for León Mondragón to ignore. That's where his path had diverged from Carmen's: she had gone forward, left her island, and made new friends, had fresh adventures far away from VILE. León had gone back to his mountain and vanished — into thin air.

"I understand him," Carmen said slowly. "And I don't understand him. We were alike, but we ended up different." Carmen bowed her head and added, "I was luckier."

She lifted her head. It felt heavy, weighed down by all the feelings that had tormented León Mondragón so many centuries before. The light of her headlamp bounced off the cavern's jagged walls.

"What was that?" she asked in a hushed voice. She scanned the side of the cavern again, nodding her head up and down so that her light hit the same spot it had a moment ago. She stepped closer.

If she tilted her headlamp at exactly the right angle, she could just make out something carved in the rockface. Two words:

¡ARRIBA!
LIBERTAD

Carmen recognized León Mondragón's handwriting. That was a good sign — he had definitely been in this spot. But what did his message mean? *Arriba* was something people shouted at sports matches, kind of like shouting "Charge!" at a ballgame. *Libertad* meant freedom. Carmen was totally stumped. Why would Mondragón had carved those words? Maybe they were meant to encourage downtrodden miners.

Suddenly, Carmen felt angry at Mondragón for leading her all the way here with nothing but a rudimentary map and two completely opaque words. *What was he trying to tell her?*

The humming sound filled the cavern again; it was coming closer, and for just a moment Carmen remembered her old fantasy that a miner was singing somewhere in another channel — and then the sound came still closer, and Carmen's stomach clenched.

That was no angelic singing she had been hearing.

It was coming down the wide gallery, louder now, undistorted by the echoes of the mine. And it was sinister.

In spite of herself, Carmen gasped as El Topo jumped over the stationed cart and landed in the cavern, closely followed by Le Chèvre. Arms swinging, Paperstar came down behind them and settled herself into one of the carts, legs hanging off the side as if it were a beanbag chair.

El Topo and Le Chèvre were very close to her; there were certainly no more than two inches between each of them. Carmen calculated her options and her hands felt suddenly sweaty. There were only two ways out—one of them was blocked by Paperstar's lounging form, and the other was so narrow and tight that Carmen could not possibly escape fast enough. If she tried, she would be dragged back in an instant—and worse still, she was no closer to finding the lion than she had been when she entered the mine.

"How did you get here?" Carmen said in what she hoped was a thoroughly fearless voice. "Kalamazoo didn't suit you?"

Paperstar sneered from her cart. "We didn't fall for your little trick, Black Sheep. As soon as we landed in Kalamazoo and saw the headlines—"

"So you did fall for the trick, otherwise why would you have gone to Kalamazoo?"

"The weather is quite lovely this time of year," Paperstar replied. "Your little friends didn't even think to divide and conquer," she went on tauntingly. "Both huddled on one side of the mountain—*hello*, it's *a circle!*"

"Technically it's a cone," Carmen clarified. She didn't know why she was picking geometry fights with Paperstar, except that she didn't know the last time she had been in such a compromised position, and if she were going to be pitched down a mine shaft by VILE, she would rather have the satisfaction of telling off Paperstar first.

But before Carmen could think of any other snide remarks, El Topo and Le Chèvre grabbed her by each arm and lifted her off the ground. Her hardhat banged on the ceiling. She struggled but they had a firm grip on her, and in an instant they were heaving her body over the carts. She kicked and writhed, wondering what they were planning, turning her face left and right to keep from being banged up by the metal carts—*always protect the face*—a voice inside her said, and then finally one of her kicks landed home and El Topo yowled in pain, letting go of Carmen and falling spread-eagle on his back, a foot from the cart. Carmen hurled herself into a midair flip, forcing Le Chèvre to let go if he didn't want to somersault with her. She landed belly over the bottom cart, foot braced against the heavy rock that held the carts in place. Le Chèvre and El Topo were both growling and crawling back toward the carts, eager to take another swing at Carmen, but Paperstar was idly folding an origami lotus flower. Her face was bottom-lit by Carmen's headlamp, like a garish jack-o'-lantern.

"Don't worry, boys," Paperstar said cheerfully, "there's nowhere for her to go but down."

In spite of herself, Carmen sneaked a peek behind her, and what she saw made her stomach lurch. Below this cavern, the tunnel took a sharp dive. If she were to lose her grip, she would have no hope of stopping her fall until she hit the bottom — and by the looks of it, the bottom was a long way off. Carmen gulped. Her hands were growing sweaty, and Le Chèvre and El Topo would recover from their injuries in about a second. Even her grappling hook couldn't save her if gravity were pushing her down, down, down . . .

Carmen pursed her lips, wishing suddenly she could talk to Player, or Ivy, or Zack — anyone who knew her and cared about her — just for a moment. But she wouldn't give Paperstar the satisfaction of knowing she was scared. She wouldn't say a word into her comm-link earring.

Things were looking very bad, indeed. Even if she called for help now, Zack and Ivy would never get to her in time. VILE had no reason to show her mercy — once Carmen had plunged to her death, they would have all the time in the world to search the cavern. *They* didn't care about the exhibit opening, they would dig up every inch of it with time to spare. And it was Carmen who had led them down here.

She glanced up one more time, at Le Chèvre, who was climbing over the edge of one of the carts, at El Topo, still nursing his injured leg, and at Paperstar, starting calmly on her second lotus.

Perhaps it was Carmen's imagination, but for a split

second, she saw something that seemed almost like a glimmer of daylight—something definitely sparkled above her—and for one irrational moment, Carmen felt a tickle of hope. Maybe she would see the sky again.

And then it dawned on Carmen, quite suddenly: *arriba.* It didn't just mean "Charge!"—if you weren't at a sports game it could also just mean "upward." Maybe León Mondragón meant that *literally.* After all, what León Mondragón had yearned for when he was in Spain, angry at the Spanish and at the merchant Joaquín Reinoso, was home and freedom. For Mondragón, home was *up,* up in the mountains. Carmen almost shouted with joy because in a rush she realized that the glimmer she had seen above her wasn't her imagination, but a real sparkle. She knew, deep in her bones, where the lion was buried.

It was risky, but she loosened one arm, letting herself dangle off the edge of the cart. "Hey, Paperstar," she called. "What if I don't care if I fall down here? What if I was headed that way anyway?"

Paperstar raised an eyebrow. "Then I would think you would want a cart so you didn't break your neck, wouldn't you?"

"That's right," Carmen said. "I would like a cart. Care to lend me this one?" With effort, she threw her arm over the edge again, and though her abdominal muscles screamed in pain, she managed to throw herself a little more securely into the cart. Now her head was facing down into the cart, and her stomach was flopped over the edge. One foot still touched the rock beneath her. It was a ridiculous position, but her heartbeat slowed now that the chance of slipping into an abyss seemed slightly less likely.

"I think not," Paperstar said, but she glanced at Le Chèvre and El Topo, and in that instant, Carmen knew she had them. She reached one arm down — it didn't quite reach the rock, but she had her foot there.

"I might take a ride anyway," Carmen said. "I really don't need your permission."

Then everything happened all at once. Le Chèvre and El Topo leaped into the cart next to Paperstar, their greedy eyes fixed on Carmen. They thought she was going to take them to the silver lion, somewhere in the pitch-black depths. But with a kick and a yell, Carmen loosened the stone and half rolled, half jumped over the edge of the cart. She cut herself in what felt like a million places as her body bumped over the metal, but Carmen didn't care. She landed flat on her stomach with lungs full of dust, but the cart rushed by her, gathering speed with gravity, sending the three VILE operatives down, deep down, into a tunnel where Carmen was sure no light would reach them.

She scrambled to her feet and reached for her hardhat

and headlamp, both of which had fallen off. Every muscle in her body was aching, but she climbed a few steps to where the wide gallery's steep slope met the little cavern, and sure enough, just where things pointed up, out of the cavern, she found a tiny *x* etched in the ground. And jutting out of the rocky dirt, a glimmer of silver.

CHAPTER 26

THE LINE WAS WRAPPED AROUND THE PLAZA and loud with joy. Everyone was talking excitedly and craning their necks for a view of the entrance. Milly's family was gathered round the door—guests of honor. They beamed at Carmen, who was dressed in her very best clothing.

Then the doors of the museum opened, and the crowd parted. With a little push from Ivy, Carmen walked slowly down the tunnel of people—only this tunnel didn't feel narrow, or dark, or cramped—it was light and full of freedom. Carmen was walking down it because she very much wanted to bring her new friend Milly the treasure hidden in her pocket.

Two guards in official uniforms held open the doors, and Carmen and Milly thanked them. Inside, the Casa de la Moneda was full of arches and tan and red bricks that reminded Carmen of Sevilla. For better and for worse, these two places were connected. Potosí had brought Carmen people like León Mondragón and people like Milly—people who knew what it was to be not just from one place, but from many. The thought cheered Carmen. After all, if Milly could be Spanish and Bolivian and a New Yorker all rolled into one, maybe she would turn out to be more than just VILE—maybe she came from more stories than she knew just yet.

Carved at the top of the central arch was a face, laughing merrily, with grapes woven into its hair. Below, the Throne of Felipe shone in all of its silver and mahogany magnificence.

Carmen handed Milly the package tucked safely in her pocket. When the wrappings fell away, Milly held a gleaming silver lion. Its fur looked real enough to touch, and its roar was frankly terrifying. Carmen couldn't fathom how a person could make something look so *alive,* but she appreciated it. She had a feeling a lot of other people would too.

"You should do this with me," Milly said, and she and Carmen knelt at the base of the throne in unison.

The silver lion fit perfectly in the spot the carpenter had left for it, many centuries before. All three shapes gleamed together: lion, castle, and arrow. To some, they might represent the mightiness of the Spanish Empire.

But to Carmen and Milly, they represented the work of a passionate mestizo artisan. And they were beautiful.

"I think," Milly said, "that a change of name might be in order. How about you?"

Carmen nodded eagerly, and with a joyous laugh, Milly reached for the tented card that served as a hastily made exhibit guide. Where it said "The Throne of Felipe," Milly crossed it out and now wrote in her own hand "The Throne of León—*y de todos nosotros.*"

"Now let's go get everyone," Milly said, pulling Carmen into a hug as the doors were thrown open, and the people flooded the exhibit with their *ooh*s and *aah*s of admiration. Everything was as it was meant to be.